IT TAKES MORE THAN GOOD GRADES TO GRADUATE FROM CENTRAL ACADEMY . . .

Discover the chilling adventures that shadow the halls and stalk the students of
TERROR ACADEMY!

LIGHTS OUT

School reporter Mandy Roberts investigates the suspicious past of the new assistant principal. The man her widowed mother plans to marry . . .

STALKER

A tough punk comes back to Central with one requirement to complete: vengeance . . .

SIXTEEN CANDLES

Kelly Langdon discovers there's ~~more to being~~ popular than she thoug~~ht~~

D1221984

This book also co~~ntains~~ the next exciting book in the TERROR ACADEMY series by Nicholas Pine: **THE NEW KID.**

TERROR ACADEMY
SPRING BREAK

NICHOLAS PINE

BERKLEY BOOKS, NEW YORK

SPRING BREAK

A Berkley Book / published by arrangement with
the author

PRINTING HISTORY
Berkley edition / September 1993

ISBN: 0-425-13969-7

A BERKLEY BOOK ® TM 757,375
Berkley Books are published by The Berkley Publishing Group,
200 Madison Avenue, New York, New York 10016.
The name "BERKLEY" and the "B" logo
are trademarks belonging to Berkley Publishing Corporation.

PRINTED IN THE UNITED STATES OF AMERICA

10 9 8 7 6 5 4 3 2 1

For Peter and little Mark

ONE

Laura Hollister lowered her dark brown eyes to the first question of her Honors English examination. As her pretty face bent toward the page, a lock of thick, black hair fell over her high cheekbones, blocking her vision for a moment. She brushed back the unruly tresses, sighing and frowning at the black printing. Laura had studied hard for the exam, the last test before spring break, which signaled a temporary end to homework, pop quizzes, term papers, and tardy bells. Unlike most of the students at Central Academy, though, Laura wasn't looking forward to spring break.

"Is something wrong, Miss Hollister?"

Laura glanced up to see her teacher, Mr. Frankland, staring at her. His sharp tone had forced everyone else in the class to look up at Laura. Mr. Frankland was Laura's least favorite teacher, though she pretended to like him because she didn't want him to be angry with her.

1

"Uh, no, everything is fine, Mr. Frankland."

But he would not let it rest. "You know, Miss Hollister, that this test counts as half your grade for the second semester."

"Yes, sir."

"Then I suggest you get to work."

"Yes, sir."

She peered down at the paper again, a distressed expression on her pale face. Laura was an attractive girl with a pert, upturned nose that at first glance gave her the appearance of snobbishness. But the smile that was often on her full lips and her hearty laugh told anyone that she was basically a good-natured person. Today, however, she was filled with dread at the onset of the two-week hiatus that came at the end of March.

The first question was on *Julius Caesar*, the Shakespearean tragedy that they had read back in February: Why did Brutus want to kill Caesar?

Laura wrote down, "To preserve the republic." She studied the answer for a moment, then decided it wasn't enough for Mr. Frankland so she added, "Brutus feared the crowning of Caesar as emperor." That should do it, she thought.

Her intelligence took over, allowing Laura to forget her woeful musings. She began to breeze through the questions, her pencil blazing. Mr. Frankland always gave short answer and essay questions, preferring that format to multiple choice. Difficult classes were a fact of the honors program at Central, the best school in the Port City area. Anyone who graduated from

Central Academy had a good chance of being accepted to a good college.

Laura reached the essay question before anyone else in the class. It was about *The Old Man and the Sea*, the short novel by Ernest Hemingway. Laura took her time answering the question but she still finished the exam in forty minutes, leaving twenty minutes until the bell rang. Even after she had rechecked all her answers, a full fifteen minutes remained on the clock.

Laura sighed again and leaned back in her chair. The break loomed before her, a grim reminder of what was to come. How could her parents do this to her? She was sixteen! Soon to be seventeen, which meant that she was almost an adult. Didn't she have a say in the way she lived her own life?

Putting down the pencil, she let her eyes wander to the casement of the window. It was a dreary March day outside. A dull, gray sky formed an ugly ceiling over Port City. She could see gulls and terns riding the air currents as they swooped down toward the Tide Gate River. The seabirds were free, she thought, not a prisoner like her.

"Miss Hollister?"

She looked up at Mr. Frankland's soda-bottle lenses. "What?"

"Are you finished?"

She said, "Yes, sir."

"Even the last question?" he challenged.

"Yes, the one about *The Old Man and the Sea*."

He chuckled. "No, look on the back of the page."

Rolling her eyes impatiently, she flipped over the exam paper to see the question that was marked "Just For Fun: What do you plan to do on your spring break?" Mr. Frankland was always trying to be amusing, though his "Just For Fun" questions were far from entertaining.

Laura blushed and tried to smile. "Oh, I'm sorry, I—"

"It's all right," he replied. "You still have ten minutes."

Laura knew she had to answer the question even though it was silly. If she didn't attempt some kind of response, it might offend Mr. Frankland and thereby affect her final grade. She had a perfect average at Central. She didn't want to blow it just because she was in a bad mood.

What *do* I expect from my spring break? she wondered.

In an almost involuntary gesture, her pencil began to move, writing one word: *Disaster!*

No! That wouldn't do. It was the kind of response that would make him angry and force him to nitpick on every one of her answers.

Disaster!

It was true enough, she thought, but she couldn't put that down. She erased it and wrote something about enriching her studies at the library, even if that wasn't what lay ahead. It was the kind of answer Mr. Frankland lived for.

When the bell rang, Laura slid out from behind her desk, moving toward Mr. Frankland.

She dropped the test paper on his desk and headed for the door. When he called to her, she ignored him and just kept going. She had other things on her mind. And they all spelled one word.

Disaster.

The halls of Central Academy were uncharacteristically wild and raucous with the onset of spring break, as though a lunatic asylum had unleashed the inmates for a day of total chaos. Laura moved toward her locker, dragging her heels amidst the joyous tumult of her classmates. All of the juniors attended classes in the same building, one of three structures that housed the classrooms for grades nine through twelve.

Laura wished she could share in some of the merriment but the feeling just wasn't there. Sure, she looked like any other student in the junior class. She wore a blue-hooded parka over her jeans, a Central Academy T-shirt, and new running shoes. With her tall, slender frame and cover-girl looks, she was one of the most sought after girls for Friday night dates. Guys were always asking her out. Her heart, however, belonged to her boyfriend.

Pausing in front of her locker, she put her head against the door and stood there, wishing that she could just die. Maybe there was a way. No, it was set. She was stuck, with no escape.

Disaster!
Gloom and doom!

Misery to the max!

"Hey, gorgeous, what's with you?"

She felt a hand on her shoulder. Laura turned to look into the eyes of Charlie Sherwood, her boyfriend. His handsome face was all smiles and happiness, just like the other members of the junior class.

Laura sighed dejectedly. "Hi, Charlie."

"You don't look happy."

"I'm not."

"Maybe this will make you feel better."

He took her face in his hands, lowering his lips to hers in a sweet kiss. They had been going steady since Christmas. Charlie was a nice guy, really cute with green eyes, sandy hair, and a runner's build. He wasn't a jock, even though he ran cross-country for the Central track team. He also studied hard so he'd get into a good college after graduation.

Laura broke away from the kiss. "Not now."

Charlie frowned. "What's wrong?"

"I don't know," she replied. "I'm just down."

Charlie laughed. "Down? This is the greatest. School's out. We're free. I love it, babe."

"I know, I know," Laura sighed.

"We've got two whole weeks together. It's gonna be hot. I'm stoked. You should be too."

She leaned back against the locker, trying to smile. Charlie was so sweet. She hadn't told him yet. She hadn't told anyone except her best friend, Kimmy. How was she going to break the news to the only boy she had ever loved? It might split them up forever when he found out.

Charlie put his hand on her soft cheek. "Laura, this is going to be special. You know what I mean? We've been talking about it all winter. You and me finally . . ."

"Charlie, don't start with this right now, okay?"

"But I thought—"

"I know what you think. That's all you ever think about."

He pulled his hand away. "I love you, Laura. And I thought you loved me."

Laura exhaled, making a defeated sound. "I do love you, Charlie. But I can't think about this right now. Okay?"

His green eyes narrowed into an expression of genuine concern. "What's wrong, babe?"

"Charlie . . ."

How was she going to tell him? Would it ruin everything? They had come so far together. Their relationship had been growing every day. Charlie had promised to give her a pre-engagement ring as soon as he got it from the jeweler.

"Laura, you can tell me anything. You know that."

"Charlie, I need time to think."

He took a step backward, grimacing in that impatient way boys had when they were confounded by girls. "Think about what?"

Laura heard the little voice in the back of her mind, articulating her worst fears. She saw the other girls descending on Charlie, taking him away from her. She heard their laughter, imagining Charlie as he chose the most beautiful girl in Port City. The girl who would give him exactly what he wanted. . . .

"I'm not sure, Charlie. I mean, we're moving too fast. I think we should wait awhile. Until we're more sure."

Charlie reached out again, stroking the long, black tresses that fell onto Laura's shoulders. "I am sure. I love you."

"Oh, Charlie, I love you too. But . . ."

His hand fell to his side. "But! It's always but! It's always going to be but, isn't it?"

"Not forever," Laura replied.

How could she tell him what was really wrong? It didn't seem to matter. Either way he was going to be angry. She would ruin their spring break in a single moment.

Charlie took a deep breath, shaking his head. "I'm sorry, Laura. It's just—I get crazy when I'm with you. I've never felt like this about anybody."

Laura threw her arms around his waist, hugging him tightly. She never wanted to let go of him. Why did love have to be so complicated? She didn't seem to have any choice but to tell him the truth and risk losing him.

Charlie hugged her back. "What is it, Laura?"

She began to cry. The words wouldn't come. She kept seeing him surrounded by other girls. She could feel him slipping out of her life.

He pushed her gently away from him, peering into her teary eyes. "Are you okay?"

She shook her head. "No."

"Laura, tell me what's wrong."

She hugged him again, thinking that she had to have faith in him. If he really loved her, he would understand. He had to understand.

Charlie stroked the back of her head. "Hey, I know. Let's go out tonight. Maybe a burger and a movie."

Laura drew back. "I can't, Charlie. Not tonight."

He grimaced again, shaking his head, turning away. "I can't take much more of this, Laura. Either you tell me what's wrong or I'm out of here."

"Charlie, please—"

He threw up his hands. "Why can't you tell me what's—"

A voice rose suddenly behind them, cutting through the noise of the hallway celebrations. "Hey guys, how about it? Fourteen days of freedom. We finally made it!"

Kimmy Anderson, Laura's best friend, moved next to them. She smiled, not realizing they were having a fight. Kimmy's short-cropped blond head bobbed up and down happily.

"Par-tay," Kimmy went on, her blue eyes flashing. "We're ready to rock and roll. Just like the big kids."

Charlie's eyes were still locked on Laura's sad face. "Some of us are big kids, Kimmy. The rest of us want to stay in the sandbox."

Laura's frown turned into an angry scowl. "That's not fair, Charlie. I told you—"

"That's right," he replied. "You told me. You told me all I need to know. Give me a call if you ever decide to grow up."

He started away from her, storming off down the hall.

Laura took a step after him. "Charlie, wait!"

Kimmy's smooth face turned bright red. She was a small pixie of a girl, cute, but short and skinny. She and Laura had been best friends since third grade. Kimmy felt terrible, thinking that she had somehow caused the fight.

"Laura, I—"

Laura sighed and wiped her eyes. "Oh, it's all right, Kimmy. It's not your fault."

"Ooohhh," Kimmy replied, her eyes widening in sudden understanding. "You told him."

Laura shook her head. "Worse. I didn't tell him. I couldn't find the words. They just wouldn't come out."

Kimmy sighed and shook her head. "Wow, he went ballistic over nothing?"

"Not really. I mean, it wasn't exactly over nothing."

Kimmy knew immediately what Laura was talking about. They had discussed it many times. Kimmy had often wished she had her own boyfriend problems, but she hadn't been so lucky—yet. She had been living vicariously through Laura, often wishing that Charlie was her boyfriend.

"Maybe you should just tell him," Kimmy offered. "Get it over with. That might be best."

Laura spun around to open her locker. "Yeah, right. Then I've lost him for good."

"Oh, I don't know," Kimmy replied, straightening the folds of her wraparound denim skirt. "I mean, hasn't Charlie always been a good guy? He's not like the other boys. He's sweet, isn't he?"

Laura stared into the mess of her locker. "I thought he was. Maybe he really is just like the others. After one thing and one thing only."

Kimmy leaned back against the lockers, gazing off dreamily into space. "I wish some guy was after anything I got."

"What am I going to do, Kimmy?"

Kimmy shrugged. "Tell him. Otherwise, you're going to blow it."

"What if I already have?"

"Then it doesn't matter," her best friend replied. "Just do it. What have you got to lose?"

"I don't know . . ."

"Do you love him?"

Laura nodded. "You know I do."

"Then tell him now, before it's too late."

Laura slammed the locker door. She didn't want anything in there. She wanted Charlie.

"You're right, Kimmy."

"I'm always right! Now go!"

Laura had to be with her boyfriend.

To give him the awful news.

Disaster.

TWO

Laura tried to run through the hall but the throng of students impeded her progress. She kept bumping into people and was almost knocked down a couple of times. Charlie was heading for his car in the junior parking lot. He had saved enough money the previous summer to buy a used Subaru GL hatchback. Laura had to catch him before he was out of reach.

She slammed into a wild-eyed boy who grabbed her shoulders. "Hey, babe, how about a spring break kiss?"

Laura pushed him away, into the wall of lockers. "Creep," she said.

The boy only laughed as she walked away. "Wait till I'm a senior, babe. You won't turn me down then!"

Laura ignored him. She had to find Charlie. She was gripped by the desperate fear that she might lose him forever. They couldn't break up over a stupid misunderstanding. She owed it to

13

Charlie to be truthful with him. The truth might even bring them back together and make their relationship stronger.

Laura burst through the doors at the end of the hallway. She gazed toward the gymnasium and the pool dome, searching the Central campus. Charlie was nowhere to be seen. She turned toward the junior parking lot, sprinting as fast as her legs would carry her.

Pausing at the edge of the junior lot, she scanned the cars, looking for Charlie's Subaru. She saw him get into the car, climb behind the wheel, and slam the door.

"Charlie, wait!" she cried.

She bolted toward the car, almost bouncing off the fender of a Toyota. The driver honked the horn and waved a fist at her. Laura ignored his outburst, weaving between the vehicles to get to Charlie. The Subaru was starting to move toward the street, following the line of cars that fled from the Central campus to enjoy two weeks away from the rigors of study.

"Charlie!"

Laura caught him before he could leave. She put her hands on the car door, startling him. He turned his head to glare at her.

"Charlie, don't leave yet. I have to talk to you."

He sighed and shook his head. "I can't play these games, Laura. I—"

"Please, I'll tell you the truth. Just don't run

away. I don't think I could stand it if we broke up."

Charlie's face went blank. "Break up? Who said anything about breaking up? Laura, I—"

A car horn blared behind them.

"Hey, Sherwood," the driver called, sticking his head out the window. "Get that crate moving. School's out, man. We're free at last."

Charlie poked his head out and yelled, "Hold your water, Thompson."

"Come on, Sherwood!"

"Chill out, I'm talking to my girl."

Laura clung tightly to the car, trying to catch her breath in the cold air. Other cars were starting to honk, but Laura didn't care. She had to square things with Charlie.

Disaster supremo!

Charlie's face softened a little. "You're still my girl, aren't you?"

Laura nodded. "Charlie, please . . ."

The entire parking lot was a symphony of car horns.

Charlie sighed. "Better get in before everybody has a cow."

Laura jumped in on the passenger side. Charlie put the car in gear and roared out of the lot. Laura reached over and took his hand, clinging tightly to him. She still wasn't sure how she would tell him.

Charlie looked sideways at her. "Something's really wrong, isn't it?"

"Just keep driving."

Laura was trying to compose herself. It wasn't going to be easy. Spring break, she thought. More like spring breakup!

Charlie turned down Rockbury Lane, steering toward Fair Common Park. Port City was starting to come to life with the promise of spring. The quaint, seaside New England town would soon be completely thawed, bringing the first blossoms of iris and daffodil. It was going to be a great spring break—for everyone but Laura.

"Where are we going?" Charlie asked.

Laura closed her eyes. "I don't care. Just give me a minute."

They had never fought before. How would she tell him? Just blurt it out, she thought. But what if it ended their relationship for good?

Charlie felt a little apprehensive. He was starting to fear the worst. He had never seen Laura so upset. Sure, she had been a little nervous all week, but Charlie had written it off as pre-exam nerves.

"I'll head for the beach," he told her. "It might be a little cold but everyone will—"

"Fine."

They were quiet as Charlie guided the Subaru through the center of Port City. It was an old town, full of American history and New England heritage. The clock in North Church, where George Washington had once worshipped, struck the half hour as they glided through Market Square. Charlie turned onto the beach access road, heading toward Hampton Way and the Atlantic Ocean.

"What's wrong?" he asked as they wound along the curvy road, away from town. "Is it exams? I'm sure you did fine. I mean, you studied harder than I did."

"No, it isn't exams."

"Then what?"

She took a deep breath. "I . . . oh, Charlie." She squeezed his hand.

"What?"

Laura gazed ahead, her eyes on the road. They were almost at the entrance for the beach park. She told Charlie to pull into the parking lot. She wanted to walk out to Agony Bluff. It might be easier to tell him there.

Charlie parked the car in an empty lot that would be full in a couple of hours with students celebrating the two weeks off. They got out and walked through a small area of withered natural growth that had been protected by the state. The entire coastal region around Port City was a sanctuary for the seabirds and marine life that used the inlets of the estuary.

Laura held his hand as they emerged onto the rocky area known as Agony Bluff. In the early days of clipper ships and whaling vessels, the wives of sailors and whaling men had waited on the bluff, anxiously wondering if their husbands would ever return from the cruel, cold northern seas. At least those wives had some faint glimmer of hope. Laura had run out of hope. But she still had to tell him.

An icy wind whipped off the ocean as the waves crashed against the rocks below the bluff. Laura's hair swirled around her shoulders. She turned to face Charlie, looking into his green eyes.

Charlie smiled, momentarily forgetting their problems, and took both of her cold hands. "You're so beautiful."

Laura sighed. She didn't really think of herself as beautiful, just healthy and non-ugly. It was part of the charm that had drawn Charlie to her.

"Charlie, I—"

He didn't let her finish. Instead, he wrapped her in his warm arms, kissing her for a long time. Laura returned the kiss, thinking it might be their last. Finally they broke off.

"Charlie, about spring break. I know we talked about—"

He laughed. "Hey, I was out of line. I don't care about *that*. I care about *you*."

"That's so sweet."

Charlie lifted his arms in a sweeping gesture to the sea. "We're as free as the fish and the birds. This is going to be the best spring break ever."

"No," Laura replied weakly. "It's not."

A dubious glint flashed in his green eyes. "What?"

"That's what I've been trying to tell you,

Charlie. We won't be together during spring break," she said.

His expression turned bitter and angry. "You're breaking up with me, aren't you? You're blowing me off. What is it? Some other guy?"

She grabbed his hands tightly, trying to convince him. "No, Charlie, it's nothing like that. I love you. You're the only one for me. You know that."

"Don't play games with me, Laura," Charlie said.

"Okay, okay. Here it is." She braced herself. "I have to go away. I won't be in Port City during spring break."

All of the anger seemed to drain out of him. "Going away? Where?"

She turned to look out at the roiling water, unable to face him. "To northern Maine. My father has taken a cabin for two weeks. I have to go with my family. They won't have it any other way."

"But your father works at the shipyard," Charlie said. "He's like an architect or something."

"An engineer," Laura corrected. "And he's taking some of his work with him. He thinks we all need to get away."

Charlie was stunned. "Incredible. I don't believe it."

Laura closed her eyes, feeling the biting wind on her cheeks. "I don't believe it either."

"Bummer. Double bummer. *Major* bummer!"

"Now do you see why I couldn't tell you?"

Charlie put his hand on her shoulder. "How far up in Maine?"

"Moosehead Lake."

"Oh, great. Why don't they just take you to Canada? Or all the way to Alaska?"

Laura wanted to comfort him, to tell him it wouldn't be that bad. But it *was* going to be that bad. What a disaster!

Charlie voiced what she was thinking. "Moosehead Lake. Great. I'm working six days a week so that means I can't even see you on my day off. It would take me more than a day to drive up and back. And I can't quit. Mom put so much effort into getting me the dishwashing job at the restaurant."

"I know, I thought about that."

"I know why your parents are doing this," he went on. "They don't want us to be together. They think we're getting too involved. That's it, isn't it?"

Laura shrugged. "I don't know."

Charlie threw up his hands. "Your father has never liked me. And I can't figure out why."

"He likes you—"

"No he doesn't! He thinks I'm some kind of dweeb. I see the way he looks at me. Man, this bites."

"Charlie—"

"And your mother! She can't stand me either. I mean, what's wrong with me? It's not like I'm a delinquent or anything. I think I'm a pretty together guy. Okay, my mom and dad are divorced. Sure, I live in Pitney Docks, but on the east end near the water. Our house isn't a mansion, but it's not a shack either. We can't all live in Prescott Estates like your family."

Laura pulled him close to her. "It's not that, Charlie."

"Yes, it is. They don't want you hanging around with a kid whose father is gone and his mother works as as waitress."

"Charlie, please," she begged, embracing him tight.

He hugged her back. They kissed again, their lips meeting with a desperate passion. Laura felt alive in his arms. She wanted to please him, to do anything to keep him. But she felt him slipping away.

She could already hear the other girls.

"Charlie's sooo cute."

"I want him."

"Where's Laura anyway?"

"Up in some hick town in Maine."

"I bet she's dating a bear."

"Or some guy in a hunting cap!"

They'd all have a good laugh before one of them would say, *"Charlie's a hunk, so I'm going for it."*

"What about Laura?"

Another laugh, then, *"Laura who?"*

Laura drew back, gazing into his sad eyes. "Charlie, if you want to . . . I mean, maybe we should stop—"

He put his finger on her lips. "No."

"What?"

"Not like this," Charlie said. "I mean, I know we've been talking about it, but I don't want it to be for the wrong reason."

Laura felt her heart melting. Was he for real? She couldn't help but love him. He was the most special guy she had ever known.

Charlie took a deep breath and then exhaled. "Well, I guess that's it. When are you leaving?"

She had to find the strength again. "The day after tomorrow."

"What!?"

Laura found herself getting angry. "It stinks. But that's what they told me. I can't believe they would do this to me."

Charlie became hopeful for a moment. "Hey, couldn't you stay in Port City? I mean, hang out with Kimmy or something. Her parents have a big house. And you guys are best friends. Almost sisters."

Laura knew better but she said, "I could ask. I mean, I'm going to be seventeen next week. Why shouldn't I be able to do what I want? I'm almost an adult, at least by legal definition."

"Yeah."

They looked into each other's eyes. Both of them were thinking the same thing. How could they be apart for two whole weeks? How could they survive without each other?

"Laura, I love you."

"Kiss me again."

Their mouths pressed together in a warm
kiss. Their arms entwined, embracing with the
hopeless strength of ill-fated, star-crossed lov-
ers. Agony Bluff was certainly living up to its
name this cold day.

Charlie broke off and grabbed her hand.
"Come on."

"Where are we going?"

"Back to town. Hurry, I want to get there
before it closes."

"Before what—"

But Charlie was running toward the parking
lot, dragging Laura behind him. They climbed
into the car and headed for town. Charlie
seemed upbeat now, almost happy.

"What's going on?" Laura asked. "Why are
you—"

"Don't worry," he told her. "You'll see."

They were silent as they followed the beach
road back to Port City. Charlie had the accelerator pressed almost to the floor. Why was he in
such a hurry?

"Charlie, slow down!"

But he would not listen. In less than ten
minutes, they were pulling up in Market Square,
parking in a metered spot. Laura watched as
Charlie climbed out of the Subaru.

"Where are you—"

Charlie started along the sidewalk, calling
over his shoulder. "Just feed the meter. I'll be
back in a minute."

Laura opened the door and stepped onto the

sidewalk. She found a dime in the pocket of her jeans and put it into the parking meter. She waited long enough to use another dime before Charlie came back carrying something in his hand. He was grinning from ear to ear.

"You look happy," she said.

Charlie took her hand and pressed something cold and metallic into her palm. "This is for you."

Laura's brown eyes grew wide. "Charlie, this is a pre-engagement ring. Do you—?"

He dropped to one knee. "I do."

"Oh, Charlie."

"I love you, honey. Nothing will keep us apart. If I have to wait forever, I will."

She held up the gold ring, studying the tiny diamond in the fading afternoon light. "It's so beautiful."

"Not nearly as beautiful as you."

"Oh, Charlie Sherwood, get up and give me a kiss."

He rose to his feet and wrapped her in his arms, protecting her from the cold March wind. His lips warmed her.

But as they kissed, Laura could not stop thinking about what she could say to her parents to convince them to let her stay in Port City for the spring break.

THREE

Charlie's Subaru followed the winding streets of the exclusive area known as Prescott Estates, the best neighborhood in Port City. Older houses, some of them dating back to colonial times, were mixed with recent structures like the huge two-story saltbox house where Laura lived with her family. As Charlie turned onto River Run Lane, Laura was still admiring the ring that was the symbol of their undying love.

"Don't wear it out," Charlie said with a playful smile. "And don't lose it up there in the backwoods."

Laura feigned exasperation. "Oh, you! I won't lose it. And I won't break it. I promise."

Charlie braked in front of the white clapboard home. "All out for the Hollister mansion."

Laura's expression became serious. "Charlie, are you sure about this? I mean, what if you meet someone else while I'm—"

"No. There isn't going to be anyone else. Ever.

You got that? I'll be right here when you get back."

She sighed, her eyes straying back to the glint of the ring. Laura wished she could remain in Port City for the break so everyone could see that she and Charlie had made it official. She wanted all the girls to know that Charlie was strictly off limits! But there wasn't going to be time to tell them.

She felt his hand on her forearm. "How about a good-bye kiss?"

Suddenly she was in a rotten mood again. "This isn't good-bye. We aren't leaving until the day after tomorrow."

Charlie shrugged. "So we can have a lot of good-bye kisses. Hey, I'll take whatever I can get right now."

She leaned closer, pursing her lips. "Then you get this."

She kissed him again and hugged him tightly, barely able to control her emotions. Laura was transported, swept off on a magic carpet. But then she was whisked back to the ground by reality.

She had to break away for a moment. "Rats!"

"What?"

She sighed, slumping in the seat. "Everything. I can't believe they're doing this to me. How can they make me go away now?"

Charlie's mood also turned sour. "I'm going to miss your birthday too. I was hoping we

could . . . well, I guess it doesn't matter anymore."

Laura reached over, grabbing him, pulling
his face toward her. She kissed him desperately, afraid to let go. What if the two week
separation did ruin their relationship?

It was Charlie's turn to draw back. "Whoa,
careful now. If you don't watch it, I'll go into
orbit."

"What are we going to do?" Laura wondered
aloud.

"I thought you were going to talk to your
parents," Charlie offered. "Try to get them to let
you stay here."

Laura nodded, though she was not hopeful. "I
will."

"You want me to call you tonight?"

"Of course. I thought we were going out."

Charlie shrugged. "I don't know. I'm going to
lift weights tonight at the pavilion in Rye Center. I might be there till nine or nine-thirty."

"You're angry at me. I know it. Oh, it's all my
fault. I'm so sorry. I wish I could—"

"Hey, it's okay. How about another kiss to
ease the pain?"

They forgot all of their troubles when their
lips met. Laura didn't want to leave him, not
even to go to into the house. But she knew they
had to part, at least for the moment. If she
could just get her parents to listen to
reason. . . .

"I have to go in, Charlie."

"Go." He put his hands on the steering wheel, taking a deep breath. "Go on. See if I care."

"Charlie—"

He flashed a broad smile. "Just kidding. Go on, I understand."

Laura was confused and happy at the same time. She grabbed the car door handle. Charlie reached over to stop her.

She glanced back at him. "What?"

"I love you, Laura."

"I love you, too."

"I mean it," Charlie said.

"I mean it more!"

He released his grip on her and grinned. "Now get out of my car."

"Gladly."

Laura climbed out of the Subaru and stepped into her yard, closing the door behind her. Charlie put the car in gear and roared off down River Run Lane. Laura shook her head, wondering why boys had so much trouble showing their true feelings. It was clear that Charlie loved her. Why did he have to resort to such childish games to hide his emotions?

She looked at the ring again. What difference did it make? He loved her. He had proven it by trusting her with the ring. That was all that really mattered.

Laura turned toward the house, striding up the stone walkway that led to the front steps. She knew her father wouldn't be home yet from work. But her mother was there. Marge

Hollister's blue Honda Civic was parked in the driveway.

Hesitating at the front entrance with her hand on the doorknob, Laura braced herself for the confrontation. Charlie had been right about one thing—her parents weren't that fond of him. Well, it wasn't really *him*, but the relationship that had been developing. They didn't want Laura getting too involved with any boy, much less someone from Pitney Docks.

Knowing she had to face the inevitable, Laura entered the house and called for her mother. No answer. Instead, she heard the mocking call of Jim Junior, her eight-year-old brother. The spiky-haired, chubby, brown-eyed imp sprung from behind a curtain and pointed at her.

"I saw you kissing Charlie," he accused. "I'm going to tell Mom."

Laura shot him a sisterly scowl and started walking toward the back of the first floor. "Oh, shut up, you little butthead."

Jim Junior followed her, taunting her from a safe distance. "Laura's got a boyfriend, Laura's got a boyfriend."

"I mean it, Junior!"

"Laura and Charlie, sittin' in a tree, K-I-S-S-I-N-G!"

She turned back to lower a finger at him. "If you don't shut up!"

Junior made kissing noises with his slobbering mouth.

"That's it, you're dog meat, you little slime!"

Laura started after him. Junior squealed and ran for the stairs, one step ahead of his angry sister. When he bolted up the stairs, fleeing to the safety of his room, Laura stopped chasing him. They would only get in trouble if they kept fighting. Laura didn't want to be on her parents' bad side when she talked to them about letting her stay in Port City during spring break.

She was about to turn away from the staircase when she saw her younger sister, Amy, coming down the steps. Amy, who had just turned eleven, would be starting middle school next year. She was slender like Laura, with the same brown eyes. Unlike her other two siblings, Amy had light brown hair, favoring their mother. She stopped on the stairs and gave Laura a quizzical look.

"What now?" Laura asked. "Don't tell me you saw me kissing Charlie too?"

Amy shrugged. "Maybe."

"So?"

Amy's pretty face curled up into a frown of disdain. "I just don't know why you want to kiss him all the time. I mean, he's cute, but don't you get germs from all that spit?"

Laura smiled. "Don't worry, someday you'll want to kiss boys too. Where's Mom? Out back?"

"No, she's over at Mrs. Roberts' house. She's borrowing something for our trip. Have you started packing, Laura?"

"No." *And if I'm lucky, I won't have to*, she thought. "How long has Mom been over there?"

"Just a few minutes. She told me to tell you to start packing as soon as you got home," Amy said.

Laura started up the stairs. "Packing is for kids." She blew past Amy, heading for her room.

"You're gonna get in trouble!" Amy called after her.

Laura ignored her younger sister, going into her room. She had her own telephone, though it wasn't a private line like some of her friends had. Laura closed the door and dropped onto her bed, reached for the phone, and dialed Kimmy's private number.

"Kimmy's World-Famous Modeling Agency."

Laura grimaced. "Oh please!"

"I knew it was you," Kimmy replied. "So, what happened?"

Laura sighed. "We drove out to Agony Bluff."

"And?"

"Well, we kissed—"

"Big deal. Did you tell him?"

Laura's eyes began to wander around the frilly decorations of her room. "I told him."

Kimmy made a hissing noise. "Okay, I'm ready. What'd he say?"

Her eyes stopped on the picture of Charlie that rested atop her dresser. "He was really ticked off at first."

"I knew it!"

"But then we drove back to town and he got a pre-engagement ring from the jeweler. He gave it to me so I could wear it and he told me he'd wait for me, that he wouldn't even look at another girl!"

"No way!"

Laura couldn't take her eyes away from Charlie's smile. "Yup. It's all true. Just like I told you."

"He'll wait? How romantic! Oh, you're the luckiest—I hate you. Hey, I'll watch him for you, make sure he doesn't go back on his promise."

Laura sat up on her bed. "That's where you come in, Kimmy. If I play it right, I may not have to go to Maine."

"What?"

"Do you think I could stay at your house during spring break?"

There was a pause on the other end of the line. "My house?"

"Sure, you've got plenty of room," Laura replied. "And your mother likes me. If I stay here, I can be with Charlie."

Kimmy paused for a moment before saying, "Wow, I hadn't really thought about it like that. I don't know—"

Laura felt her spirits sagging, her last hopes dashed by the lack of support in Kimmy's voice. "Don't bail out on me now, Anderson!"

"No, no. Wait a minute." Laura heard Kimmy yell, "Hey, Mom, can Laura stay with us during spring break so she doesn't have to go to Maine?"

Laura crossed her fingers, awaiting the muffled answer.

Finally, Kimmy came back. "Okay. As long as you have your parents' permission."

"Great! Now comes the hard part."

"What do you think they'll say?" Kimmy asked.

Laura sighed, considering her chances. "I don't know, Kimmy. But I have to try. I just have to try."

Jim Hollister leaned over the dinner table, the dining room light reflecting on his balding head. He was a chubby, round-faced, hardworking man who seemed a bit too serious for his teenaged daughter. Still, he was a good father and Laura loved him very much, except for those times when he would not listen to her side of an argument.

"Pass the potatoes," he said in a high-pitched voice.

Laura grabbed the bowl of potatoes and handed it quickly to her father. "Would you like some more butter?" she asked with a pleasant smile.

Mr. Hollister shrugged. "Sure." He did not seem to notice his daughter's attentive manner. He didn't notice the pre-engagement ring either.

Mrs. Hollister, however, had quickly realized

that something was afoot. The slender, hazel-eyed woman with the light brown hair gazed across the table with suspicion. She had known her daughter long enough to tell when she wanted something from them. The polite act wasn't fooling her.

"Is that a new ring, Laura?" she asked her daughter.

Laura blushed. "Uh, I—"

Junior, who had been playing with his roast beef and gravy with his fork, rolled his eyes at their father. "Guess what I saw today?"

Mr. Hollister only grunted as he shoveled potatoes into his mouth.

Laura gave Junior her best *one word and I kill you* look.

Junior opened his mouth to speak, only to have Amy kick him under the table. He whined, grabbing his injured shin. Amy smiled at Laura, who nodded her thanks.

Mrs. Hollister had noticed the exchange, so she took the lead, anxious to find out what was on her older daughter's mind. "So, how did you do on your exams, Laura?"

"Oh, fine," Laura said, looking at her father. "I think I'm going to have straight A's again this year, Dad."

"Uh-huh." His eyes were focused on a trade journal from the shipyard. "That's nice, honey."

"Dad, I was thinking—"

Mrs. Hollister saw it coming. "About what, dear?"

Laura tried to keep the attention focused on her father. "Well, I'm going to be seventeen next week."

Her father looked up. "Really?"

"That's correct, Jim," Mrs. Hollister said, wondering where this conversation was leading.

"Well, seventeen, I mean, I'm practically an adult," Laura went on. "I can register to vote next year."

Mr. Hollister nodded. "Laura, that's great. You're already thinking like an adult. Don't forget to register at the courthouse when the time comes."

"I won't," Laura said quickly. "Uh, Dad—"

Junior chose the exact wrong moment to blurt out, "I saw Laura kissing Charlie today!"

Laura's eyes grew wide, but she did not give in to her anger. "It wasn't anything. I—"

Mrs. Hollister had grown tired of the pretense. "Laura, why don't you just tell us what's on your mind?"

Laura put down her fork, shifting nervously in the chair. Her father had suddenly focused on her. She noticed he had gravy on his chin.

"What is it, honey?" he asked, thinking there was something wrong.

Laura cleared her throat, ignoring her mother's accusing expression. "Well, I was talking to Kimmy today. And she's going to be all alone during spring break. She and her mother live in that great big house—"

Mr. Hollister didn't even let her finish. "No!"

"But you don't even know what I'm going to say!"

"Your father is right," Marge Hollister chimed in. "You aren't staying in Port City for the spring break."

"But—"

Junior grinned at her. "She has Charlie's ring!"

Jim Hollister exhaled and leaned back in his char. "*That's* what this is about. You want to stay with Charlie."

Laura saw her hopes going up in flames. "No, I—"

"I never did like that kid," her father went on. "I don't trust him. And I don't trust *you* around him."

"Please," Laura pleaded on the verge of tears. "Let me explain. I can stay with Kimmy—"

"No, you can't," her mother said. "Your father is right. This thing with Charlie is getting too serious. It won't kill you to spend two weeks apart."

"You can't make me go to Maine!" Laura cried. "I won't go."

"Yes, you will," her father replied. "And you'll stay in the cabin with your family. If Charlie wants to come up—"

"He can't," Laura replied. "He's going to be working six days a week."

Mrs. Hollister said, "Maybe that's for the

best. I think some time apart will do you both some good. If you—"

Laura jumped up from the table, her face red. Tears flowed down her cheeks, dripping from the end of her upturned nose. "You hate me! You both hate me!"

"No," her father said, trying to sound sympathetic. "We love you. That's why we—"

Laura ran out of the dining room, sprinting down the hallway. She took the stairs two at a time. Fleeing to the privacy of her room, she slammed the door and fell on her bed, sobbing.

They were all against her.

They wanted her to have a lousy vacation.

How could they ruin everything?

The whole spring break was going to be horrible, totally horrible.

Laura had no way of knowing just how horrible it would really be.

FOUR

"Laura, you'd better get down here. We're almost ready to go. Laura?"

Marge Hollister called upstairs to her daughter, who had waited until the last minute to start packing. Mrs. Hollister was trying to be tolerant with Laura, but she was fast running out of patience. Outside, Mr. Hollister had almost completed loading the family station wagon. They would be ready to depart for Maine in ten or fifteen minutes.

"Laura!" She would threaten to leave without her daughter, except she knew that was exactly what Laura wanted. "I mean it, young lady!"

"All right!" came the hostile reply that echoed through the house. "I'll be down in a minute."

"You'd better be!"

Upstairs in her room, Laura continued to stuff her clothes into a large, nylon sports bag. She paid little attention to what she was packing. It really didn't matter. Laura wasn't going

39

to spend two weeks in Maine, even if it meant doing something drastic.

Her eyes strayed to the bedroom window. She gazed out at the gray March sky, wondering why everyone in her family had to be so cruel to her. The gloomy weather mocked her. She touched the ring that rested on her finger. Charlie meant everything to her. Her parents meant nothing!

Laura's tortured imagination swirled with visions of Charlie among the beauties of Port City. He'd have his pick of girls who would do *anything* to make him happy. She was trying to have faith in him but he was only human—and boys played by a different set of rules entirely.

"Laura!"

It was her father calling this time.

"All right!" she bellowed, keeping alive the hostile tone in her voice.

She'd show them. They'd really be sorry that they had treated her this way. The plan hadn't formed yet in her mind, but the first glimmer of an idea was there. She'd show all of them!

"I mean it," her father added. "Now."

She sighed, zipping shut the sports bag. They hadn't even allowed her to go out with Charlie on their last night together. He had come for dinner and was forced to endure a video with the rest of the family. They had barely been able to sneak a good-night kiss as Laura walked him to the car. Even then, her mother had been watching from the window!

"Laura!"

"I'm coming, all right!"

They won't get away with it, she thought resentfully.

Pulling the sports bag onto her shoulder, Laura said good-bye to her room and to her life. No fun-filled spring break for Laura Hollister. She had to spend it with her family like some elementary school charity case.

"Laura!"

She didn't answer. Closing the bedroom door behind her, Laura shuffled down the stairs with a scowl contorting her pretty face. She didn't look at her mother, who stood next to the front door with her hands on her hips.

"Did you pack everything?" Mrs. Hollister asked.

Laura just grunted and pushed past her, stomping down the front steps. Her father stood behind the car, tying luggage to the roof rack. It was one of those huge, Chevrolet station wagons with a gas-guzzling, eight-cylinder engine. They needed the car for their big family outings. Laura had enjoyed their family vacations when she was younger, but now they seemed like purgatory to her.

Jim Hollister tried to smile. "You get everything packed?"

Laura just threw the sports bag at his feet. She wasn't ready for a cheerful father—or was it a cheerful jailer? She heard the front door slamming shut, the key turning, imprisoning her for eternity. In the meantime, her friends would be living it up in Port City, having the best spring break of their lives.

"I think I have room up top for this," Mr. Hollister said, lifting the bag to the luggage rack.

Laura wanted to be contentious. "What if it rains?" she scoffed.

But Mr. Hollister just ignored her mood, replying, "I have a tarp to cover everything. It won't get wet."

Laura sighed. She looked into the car where her brother and sister were already sitting. The wagon had a third seat that faced backwards. Amy and Junior were already buckled into the seat. At least Laura would have the other backseat all to herself on the ride to hell.

How could they do this to her? Didn't they care that she had a life? Why were they working so hard to strip her of any happiness?

Her father finished tying down the tarp that covered the roof rack. "There. That ought to hold her."

Laura rolled her eyes, wishing that lightning would just strike her and end it all. She could already see the day unfolding before her: A long drive with Junior having to go to the bathroom every five minutes, Amy whining that she was bored, and the obligatory lunch at the roadside stand where her father would act like total geek and embarrass her.

"Fun, fun, fun," she muttered to herself.

Mr. Hollister turned in her direction. "What?"

"Nothing," Laura said, as if she was suffering from chronic fatigue.

Mr. Hollister was going to give her a lecture about shaping up and losing the attitude, but a car horn honked from River Run Lane.

Laura's eyes grew wide. "Charlie!"

She ran past her father to greet the bronze Subaru.

Charlie parked at the curb and got out to say good-bye. Laura threw her arms around him. She began to cry on his shoulder.

"It's horrible," she said.

Charlie nodded, stroking her hair. "I know."

Mr. Hollister put his hands on his hips, glaring at them. He was going to say something, but his wife appeared at his side. She had just locked the door, having completed her inventory for closing up the house.

Laura peered into Charlie's serious face. "I love you."

He sighed. "Me too."

"Kiss me," Laura pleaded.

Charlie glanced over her shoulder. "They're watching."

"I don't care!" Laura grabbed his face, pulling him closer. Her lips touched his mouth. The kiss was a protest, her last way of rebelling against her parents. Charlie tried to break off but she would not let him.

On the driveway, Mr. Hollister took a step in

their direction. He would to put an end to this blatant display. His daughter wasn't going to show this kind of disrespect.

But Mrs. Hollister stopped him. "No, Jim. She's been through a lot."

Her husband grimaced. "But look at them. Didn't we raise her better than that? I mean—"

"She's a young woman," Mrs. Hollister replied. "She's not our little girl anymore."

"But, Marge, that kid is all over her."

"And vice versa," she said. "Just leave it alone. She's got two weeks to cool off and think about things. Besides, Charlie isn't that bad."

"I guess." He turned back toward Amy and Junior, both of whom were giggling in the backseat. "What are you two looking at?"

Junior made a face. "They're kissing! Yuk."

"Double yuk," Amy intoned.

Mr. Hollister pointed a finger at them. "Good. Both of you keep thinking that way."

At the curb, Charlie managed to break away from the desperate hold that Laura had on him. "Wow, that's what I call playing tonsil hockey."

"Kidnap me," Laura begged him. "I'll do anything to get away from them. Let's just get in the car and drive. We'll leave Port City and never come back."

Charlie smiled dumbly. "Gosh, you really want to get out of this."

"Like you didn't know."

He sighed and shook his head. "I can't, Laura.

I have my job. I have to help my mother. You know that."

She put her head against his chest. "I know."

The station wagon's horn blasted twice. Her father and mother had gotten into the car. They were finally ready to go on the dreary March morning.

"This is it," Charlie said.

"I'm not going," Laura insisted.

"You have to," Charlie replied.

The car horn echoed Charlie's grasp of the inevitable.

Laura looked into his eyes. "You may see me sooner than you expect."

Charlie's brow wrinkled. "What?"

Honk!

"Laura!" her mother cried from the passenger side. "Come on!"

"You better go," Charlie said.

Laura smiled in a strange way. "See you soon!"

"What?"

But she was gone, running toward the car. Charlie watched her climb into the rear seat. As the wagon backed out of the driveway, Laura waved, still grinning with that eerie expression.

Charlie waved at them. Mrs. Hollister waved back. Laura seemed to drop down into the seat.

Charlie kept watching until the station wagon rolled out of sight. Why had Laura been all smiles so suddenly? She had shifted gears in a hurry.

"Wow," Charlie muttered to himself in a moment of doubt. "I sure hope Laura doesn't do anything stupid."

The ride north lived up to Laura's worst nightmares. Her parents tried to get her out of the funky mood by being cheerful and suggesting stupid car games. Junior whined every two or three minutes about having to go to the bathroom. Amy wasn't much better, asking, "Are we there yet?" with each passing mile.

Lunch, of course, was at a roadside place called Dippy Burger. It was a tourist trap with high prices that made her father complain. Laura managed to gag down a few greasy French fries but finally had to resort to her chocolate shake for sustenance. She also flirted with the cute boy behind the counter just to make her father mad.

While they were seated at Dippy Burger, Junior started to choke on his hamburger. Mrs. Hollister managed to bring him around. His father told him to eat like a human. Amy, of course, wouldn't eat anything. She said she felt "barfy" after the long car ride.

Weren't they ever going to get there?

Laura endured her family as she made eyes at the cute counter boy. But her father had begun to laugh at her. That was it! She had been mortified enough. It was time to do something drastic. And Laura had concocted a plan.

As they loaded up again in the Dippy Burger

parking lot, Laura hatched her scheme. It came to her in a rush of mental energy. A simple idea, at least in the early stages, just two words: *Run away!*

Why not? she thought as her father steered the car back onto the interstate. She could just take off. Flee back to Port City. She could stay with Kimmy for a while. Kimmy could hide her, at least until the spring break was over. Or she could stay at Charlie's. It might work.

Laura leaned back in the seat, imagining what it would be like to be married to Charlie. They were surely meant for each other. Nothing could keep them apart. Nothing!

She let herself drift in the daydream for an hour or so before Amy began to claim that she was going to be sick.

"Oh, shut up, you little dweeb," Laura said.

Junior glanced back over the seat, a scared look on his face. "I think she's going to throw up."

Mrs. Hollister rummaged in a paper bag in the front seat. "Here, give her this soda. It'll settle her stomach."

Laura opened a can of soda and passed it to Amy who felt a little better after drinking some cola. Laura experienced a sudden pang of sympathy for her little sister. Car sickness had plagued Laura when she had been Amy's age.

She reached over to pat Amy on the shoulder. "It's going to be all right, sis. We'll be there soon. Won't we?"

Mr. Hollister sighed, gazing out the window. "I suppose. Wow, it's really starting to get woodsy up here. There's even some snow left on the ground."

Laura's eyes turned to the forest along the road. Except for the evergreens, the trees were still bare-limbed, spreading to both sides of the interstate as far as the eye could see. Patches of dirty snow dotted the spaces between the tree trunks. The small towns were getting fewer and farther between. They drove for a long time before they saw another exit.

"I think we're getting closer," Mr. Hollister said. "I wish we were on daylight savings time. It's almost two. I hope we make it before it gets dark."

Laura folded her arms, forgetting the wilderness. She was scheming about how to get away. It seemed grandly romantic, escaping to be with the one she loved. She could hide out for two weeks without them finding her.

But how would she pull off her daring departure?

She couldn't steal her father's car. Of course, she did have her driver's license, but she could not leave them stranded. Then what?

Leave the cabin, walk back to the main road, and hitchhike into some town where she could find a bus that would eventually take her to Port City, even if she had to transfer a few times. Simple! She had some funds left from her Christmas money, enough for a bus ticket.

Precious freedom!

When she got back to Port City, she would call Kimmy. They would ride out to the restaurant to surprise Charlie. Laura grinned when she thought of the shocked look on his face. How glorious it would be to spend the break together!

As Laura plotted in the backseat, her parents were busy up front. Her mother had opened a map to find the road that led to the lake. Mr. Hollister was trying to study the directions provided by the rental agent.

"Give me those," Mrs. Hollister said, taking the piece of paper from his hand. "You can't drive and read at the same time."

"Did you find the road yet?" he asked.

"I think it's 9A," Mrs. Hollister replied. "Keep looking for the exit."

They drove for a long time before they reached the exit for State Road 9A. Laura kept her eyes open when they finally pulled onto the two-lane highway. It was a narrow, poorly kept road that curved through the monolithic wall of skeletal trees that towered over them, casting shadows on the station wagon. Suddenly they were driving straight into the heart of the wilderness.

"Cool," Junior said. "I bet we see that monster."

"What monster?" Amy asked timidly.

"The Wendigo," Junior replied. "He's like

Bigfoot. Only he has sharper teeth. He can rip your guts out!"

Amy put a hand on her stomach. "Mom!"

Mrs. Hollister glared back at her grinning son. "That's enough, Junior."

Mr. Hollister squinted dubiously at the highway. "Are you sure this is the right way?"

"9A," Mrs. Hollister replied.

Laura felt a coldness in her spine. The evergreens were now blocking the light, even though there was plenty of time before sunset. She kept looking for signs of civilization but they weren't readily forthcoming. Where in the world was their father taking them?

"Ah, there," Mrs. Hollister said finally.

Laura was relieved to see the sign that read MOOSEHEAD LAKE 40 MILES.

"I told you it was the right road," Mrs. Hollister said triumphantly.

Her father gave a sigh of relief. "Wow, I wouldn't want to get lost up here," he said with a nervous laugh. "Nosiree. Spring hasn't arrived up here yet."

"Lost," Laura whispered. "No, not lost."

"The Wendigo would eat you alive," Junior offered.

Amy started to whimper. "Make him stop."

"Shut up, Junior," Mr. Hollister said.

The station wagon wound deeper into the wintry forests, following the two-lane blacktop. Laura's eyes were now opened wide as she paid close attention to the area. It wasn't exactly

Port City. She started to feel a little apprehensive about running away. What if a spring blizzard blew in?

No!

She would stick to her plan no matter what difficulties she had to face.

She didn't care if they were moving ever forward into the Maine wilderness.

Laura was going to spend spring break with Charlie, no matter what!

FIVE

The Hollister family hadn't driven five miles before the clouds rolled down from the north, blotting out the sun completely. Flurries began to fall and then heavy snow came, limiting the visibility in front of the station wagon's windshield. Even with the wipers going at full tilt, Mr. Hollister could barely see the yellow line that split the bumpy, winding road.

"Slow down," Mrs. Hollister said, gazing nervously at the heavy flakes that emptied from the black sky.

"I want to get there before dark," her husband replied.

Mrs. Hollister touched his shoulder. "Slow down, Jim, or we won't get there at all."

He eased back on the accelerator, dropping from fifty-five miles an hour to forty-five. Usually, the big car was easy to handle, but the snow made the road slick, and icy, and the trip more hazardous. The highway actually seemed to be getting narrower as they moved further into the backwoods.

Junior had his nose pressed against a foggy car window. "Wow, it never snows like this in Port City. Serious snow."

Amy made a face. "I feel sick."

Laura grew tense. Something felt different after the snow started. Her hands gripped the ridge of the front seat, her knuckles as white as a bone. In the confines of the car, she was flushed, warm, short of breath. She kept telling herself to stay calm. If she was going to find her way back to Port City, she had to be in control.

The snow kept coming steadily, but it wasn't exactly a blizzard. Amy began to cry. They had all seen snow a thousand times, but now they were on edge. A weird feeling was gnawing at Laura's nervous stomach.

Junior did his best to make things worse. "The Wendigo loves snow. He likes to eat human flesh when he—"

"Mommmm!" Amy moaned.

"Cut it out, Junior," Mr. Hollister snapped from the front seat.

Mrs. Hollister looked back at Laura. "Honey, help your sister climb over the seat. She can sit up here with me."

Laura sighed, trying to be cool in spite of the strange sense of dread that had overtaken her. "She's such a baby."

"Just do it," her father said irritably. "Damned snow."

Laura helped Amy crawl awkwardly into the front seat where she sat crying on her mother's lap.

Junior giggled as he drew a monster in the window fog. "The Wendigo like to eat little girls like Amy."

"Mom!"

Mr. Hollister gazed into rearview mirror. "You keep it up, mister, and I'm going to tan your fanny when we get to the lake."

Junior eased down into the seat, giggling.

Laura gazed out again into the snow, wondering how long it would last. She might have to delay her departure for a day or so. A shiver played through her shoulders, running down the length of her spine. Though she had seen Charlie that morning, it seemed like a week since they had been together. Was her devotion to him ebbing just because of a little spring storm in the wilderness?

No, she told herself. She wouldn't allow it to happen. She was running away as soon as she got the chance. Nothing could stop her from being with the guy she loved. Nothing!

"Are you all right, Laura?" her mother asked.

She glanced up to see Marge Hollister squinting suspiciously at her. Her mother always sensed when something was afoot. How had she learned to read Laura like a book? It was almost creepy.

"Er, I'm fine, Mom. I—"

Mrs. Hollister smiled. "Don't worry, it's going to be all right."

"Sure, Mom."

Laura's fingers turned the gold ring that felt heavy on her hand. The doubts would not go away. But she was still resolved to escape.

"Do you miss him already?" Mrs. Hollister asked, trying to make conversation.

Laura shrugged. "I guess." She didn't want to appear too eager. They couldn't catch on to her plan to bolt.

As Junior kept drawing his monsters, Amy put her head on her mother's shoulder. Mrs. Hollister stroked her daughter's hair soothingly.

Mr. Hollister reached forward to wipe the fog from the windshield. "Wow, it's really coming down. This is a lot of snow for March."

The car went into a steep curve in the road. For a moment, the back wheels fishtailed into the apex of the bend. Laura thought they were going to spin off the highway. But the radial tires caught the shoulder of the road and the station wagon spurted forward out of the turn.

Laura's stomach took a roller coaster ride. "Dad!"

Mrs. Hollister had been thrown against the locked passenger door. "Jim, for God's sake!"

Amy squealed in her mother's arms.

Junior was laughing. "Cool, Dad. Do it again!"

Mr. Hollister's face had turned white. His

hands gripped the steering wheel as he straightened out the station wagon. The momentary lapse had almost hurled them into a wreck.

"Slow down!" Mrs. Hollister cried.

"All right!" he replied, easing a little more on the throttle. "It looks like I don't have much choice."

Laura peered through the foggy windshield. She saw the truck ahead of them. It was crawling on the icy road. Her father drew closer, tailgating, riding on the truck's back bumper.

"Don't get so close," Laura said. "You're going to kill us all."

"I know what I'm doing," her father insisted. "Darn, twenty-five miles an hour. Can't he go faster than that? It's just snow."

Laura couldn't believe it when her father began to lay on the car horn. The truck driver had the right idea about going slow. It was one of those vehicles that was larger than a pickup but smaller than a semitrailer. The truck seemed to be loaded with junky furniture that had been piled high against two wooden side railings.

Honk!

"Come on, get moving!" Mr. Hollister cried.

"Jim—"

"Dad, don't be so obnoxious," Laura said.

Honk!

Beads of sweat had formed on Laura's wrinkled forehead. How could her father be so stupid? At this rate, she'd never get a chance to run away. He was going to kill her to keep her from seeing Charlie.

"I'm going to pass him!"

"Dad!"

"Jim, please—"

"Cool," Junior said from the rear seat.

Despite protests from his wife and daughter, Jim Hollister floored the throttle and roared over the double yellow line that indicated no passing. As they shot past the slow-moving truck, Laura glanced wide-eyed at the driver. She saw an orange hunting hat and a dark, gaping face. The man honked his own horn to indicate the stupidity of her father's daring maneuver.

"Dad!"

The station wagon's tires skidded for a second as the car rushed through an ice patch on the uneven highway. Mr. Hollister's eyes bulged out of his face. Had he made a mistake?

Laura thought she saw the glare of head-lights coming toward them. They were barrel-ing into a head-on collision. She covered her eyes and held her breath. Charlie's ring sud-denly felt cold. For a moment, Laura was cer-tain they would die.

The station wagon's tires caught and it straightened out, barely missing the front of the junky truck. The oncoming car rushed past them, its horn blasting in angry protest. Mr.

Hollister held steadily to the wheel, guiding them into the maw of the storm.

"Real mature, Dad!" Laura cried after she opened her eyes.

"Do it again," Junior squealed with glee.

Mrs. Hollister glared at her husband. "Don't you ever try something like that with us in the car!"

"What?" he replied. "We're all right."

"Slow down," his wife insisted.

"Marge—"

"I mean it, Jim!"

The speedometer read fifty-five again. Laura's father eased off to a more acceptable forty-five. Everyone was quiet for a long time, until they passed the sign that announced MOOSEHEAD LAKE, 15 MILES.

"See," Mr. Hollister said. "We're getting closer. We're making good time, too. We'll be there before dark."

"If you don't kill us first," Laura muttered.

Her mother shot a nasty look over the back-seat. "That's enough, Laura."

Laura grimaced. "I'm not the one who's driving like a maniac."

"All right, all right," her father said good-naturedly. "Old Dad almost caused a big snafu. But we're fine now and I promise to drive like a Boy Scout for the rest of the trip."

Mrs. Hollister gave him a cold stare. "As soon as we stop this car, I'm driving!"

"Fine by me," he replied. "How's Amy?"

"Asleep."

"Or passed out!" Laura grumbled.

Junior gawked from the rear of the car. "Hey, I have to go to the bathroom. When are we going to stop?"

"As soon as we find a gas station," Mr. Hollister said. "Whenever that it. There doesn't seem to be much up this way."

Just great, Laura thought, as she studied the snowy wilds of northern Maine. They had dragged her into the middle of nowhere to shatter her hopes of a fun break. There was nothing along the side of the highway. Occasionally they would pass a lone house or trailer in a clearing, but mostly there were only a few dirt roads leading back into the wintry forest.

Mr. Hollister kept looking at the fuel gauge on the dashboard. "Huh, I hope we find a place soon."

Mrs. Hollister, who had finally regained her composure, tried to be reassuring. "There should be a place close to the lake."

As they began to talk again, Laura drifted off into her own daydreams. She started to plan her escape, but another, more disturbing vision began to whirl in her head. It was a waking nightmare that she had suffered before.

Charlie was at a dance. There were girls around him. Good-looking girls who wanted to take Charlie away from her. They were flirting shamelessly. Laura could hear what they were saying so clearly.

"Charlie, looking good!"

"Charlie, want to dance with me?"

"Where's Laura?"

"Charlie said her parents took her off to the woods."

"That's a good place for her."

"Charlie!"

"Charlie!"

"Charlie, do you like my new miniskirt?"

Laura shuddered and sat up straight in the seat. She had to get back to Port City. A good-looking guy like Charlie wouldn't stand a chance with those loose girls at Central.

"I have to go to the bathroom!" Junior insisted again.

"Hold on," Mr. Hollister replied. "We'll be there soon enough."

They passed a sign that told them they were only five miles from the lake. Laura felt better when the snow let up a little, slowing to flurries. They drove on for another ten minutes before they rounded a corner to find a small gas station behind a sign that read, "Entering Greenville."

Mr. Hollister took a deep breath. "Finally. We were almost out of gas."

As they pulled into the tiny gas station, Laura was suddenly buoyed by the prospect of returning to civilization. She saw the pay phone on the corner of the white clapboard building. Maybe she could slip away for a collect call to Kimmy, to inform her of the escape plan.

Kimmy might be able to borrow her mother's car and drive up to get her.

"All out for Yutzville," her father joked.

They piled out of the wagon. Junior immediately ran for the rest room on the side of the convenience store which was called the Greenville Corner Market. Amy, who had come back to life, made for the sugar-laden display of snack cakes. Mr. Hollister started to pump the gas while Laura's mother followed Junior in the direction of the rest rooms.

Laura saw her chance, not necessarily to run away, but to make some preparations for the break. She hurried into the store which was deceptively spacious inside. The place even carried fresh produce, meat, dairy products, and all sorts of durable goods. It was probably the only grocery store within miles.

An older man stood behind the counter at the cash register. His face showed the deep lines of a hard life in the cold northland. Rheumy gray eyes stared back at Laura from behind thick glasses. The man just stood there, motionless, as if he was waiting for her to speak.

Laura felt a little uncomfortable. "Uh, hi. . . ."

He only nodded to her without a word.

She began to stammer awkwardly. "Uh, I was wondering—does the bus stop here?"

"Sometimes," the man replied cryptically.

When he offered nothing more she asked, "Do you have a schedule?"

"Comes through about midnight."

Her impatience was getting the better of her. "Every day?"

"Ayuh."

Good, Laura thought. Night was better. When she finally made her move, she could escape in the cloak of darkness. They wouldn't miss her until morning. By that time, she'd be back in Port City.

"Do you know where the bus goes from here?" she asked.

"Nope."

Her eyes narrowed. "What *do* you know?"

"I know I don't need a bus," the old man replied.

Laura shook her head, thinking that this rural country must be full of rubes like the storekeeper. "Can I buy my ticket now?"

"Buy it on the bus."

"What do you need a bus for, Laura?"

She winced. But it was only Amy standing next to her with a handful of Twinkies. Before she could answer her little sister's question, her mother and father came into the store with Junior between them. As they began to make inquiries about grocery shopping and other local matters, Laura slipped outside to the pay phone.

The snow was still falling lightly. Laura noticed the truck that they had passed on the road. It rolled slowly by the store, taking the curve slowly, then disappearing into the white-

ness. What had her father been thinking when
he dragged them into this forsaken land of
weirdness?

She grabbed the phone and tried to make a
collect call to Kimmy. The line was busy. Before
she could redial, her parents came out of the
store with the other two children. Laura managed to hang up without them seeing her. She
had no choice but to climb back into the car,
back into prison.

Mrs. Hollister was now behind the wheel.
"Fasten your seat belts. Here we go." They
pulled away from the store, following the narrow highway in the snow.

"Well, it looks like we're going to do all of our
shopping in Greenville," Mr. Hollister offered.

"Where's the rest of the town?" Laura asked.

Her father chortled. "That *is* the town."

It's a good thing I won't be here, Laura
thought.

Mrs. Hollister steered the car through the
flurries. She kept the speed down but as the
snow subsided even more, she let the station
wagon creep up to fifty miles an hour. She was
as anxious as her husband to get to the cabin
while it was still daylight.

Laura knew the real adventure wouldn't be-
gin until after dark, when she climbed on the
bus to Port City. It was going to difficult in the
cold, but she figured she could pull it off. She
had been hiking in the winter before.

The station wagon continued barreling down

the slippery road. This time it was Mr. Hollister who cautioned his wife to slow down. She kept going, assuring him that they would be fine.

But as they went into a wide turn, Laura saw the junk-truck pulling from the shoulder of the road, lumbering straight into their path.

"Mom!" Laura cried.

Mrs. Hollister slammed on the brakes, locking up the wheels on the snowy highway.

The car began to spin round and round, out of control.

SIX

Everyone was screaming as the Hollister's car careened past the junk-truck, barely missing the front end by inches. The heavy station wagon rotated three more times and then skidded sideways on the slippery blacktop. It finally slid onto the shoulder of the road into some loose gravel. The gravel slowed the momentum enough for the vehicle to drop one back wheel into a ditch. It stalled there, leaving the family stunned but alive.

Mr. Hollister quickly took inventory from the passenger seat. "Is everyone okay? Junior?"

Laura's little brother didn't think this was so cool anymore. Amy sat next to him in the rear seat, whimpering. Laura's eyes were wide. She could not believe that her mother had almost killed them. Mrs. Hollister was slumped against the wheel with her mouth agape.

"Are you all right, Marge?" Mr. Hollister asked.

"Yes, I . . . what happened?"

Mr. Hollister reached for the door handle. "That idiot pulled out in front of us. It wasn't your fault, Marge. I'm going to give him a piece of my mind."

He unhooked his seat belt and started to get out of the car.

Laura followed him, worried that he would overreact to the situation. It hadn't been anyone's fault, not really. The truck had pulled out unexpectedly, but her mother had also been going too fast.

"Dad, wait!"

The junk-truck had stopped, resting in the middle of the highway. Two men had gotten out. When Laura saw them, she hesitated, peering at their unkempt shapes. They wore old, ratty clothes and bright orange hunting caps. Hadn't there only been one of them before? Maybe the driver had stopped to pick up a friend.

They seemed so . . . *menacing*. The word just popped into her head. They looked rough: unshaven, dirty, and low-browed with narrow eyes. They glared at her father as he ran toward them waving his arms.

"Are you crazy?" he railed at them. "You just pulled out in front of us without so much as a—"

Mr. Hollister stopped in midsentence. He had finally noticed the strange way the men were looking at them. No, not at them—at *her*. Their dark eyes were fixed on the comely girl with the upturned nose.

"Dad, don't yell at them," Laura said. "They—"

A chill shot through Laura's body. Their slitted eyes made her feel crawly all over. They seemed so calm. They had almost been in an accident but neither one of them appeared to be worried. They just stood there in front of the truck, staring at her, their breath fogging in the frigid air.

Mr. Hollister's anger came back. "Look here, you almost caused a horrible wreck. What do you have to say for yourselves?"

The driver did not reply. Instead, he turned his sooty countenance toward the other man, who seemed to be younger. They didn't talk but there was some unspoken communication between them.

Laura ran up next to her father, taking his arm. "Dad, it's okay. I'm sure they didn't mean it."

Mr. Hollister was squinting at them. "Don't just sit there like a bump on a log. At least say you're sorry."

The younger man ignored him, suddenly smiling at Laura. He took off his orange cap, revealing a greasy pate of matted hair. "How do, miss." He was missing three teeth.

Laura couldn't shake the cold sensation that had frozen her marrow. These two morons didn't even blink as they regarded her with a predatory intensity. She had to get herself and her family away from them.

"Dad, let's just go."

Mr. Hollister would not back off. "Not until they apologize."

The younger man took a step toward Laura. "I'm Jacob. This is my paw, Caleb. How do, miss."

Laura grimaced, easing away toward the car, trying to drag her father with her. "Dad, it doesn't matter."

Caleb spoke for the first time in a high, gruff voice. "Don't you like my boy, missy?"

Mr. Hollister's face had turned red. "Look here, I won't have you talking that way to my daughter."

The son glanced back to nod at the father. Caleb started to move toward the passenger side of the junk-truck. Laura kept tugging at her father who still wouldn't budge.

"Dad—"

"It was their fault," Mr. Hollister insisted.

The boy grinned his toothless smile at Laura. "We own this truck, miss. Paw and me are—" His brow wrinkled as he thought of the correct words. "Used dealers—no, dealers in used furnishin's." He nodded and straightened his body as if he thought this information would impress Laura.

For a moment, Laura was overcome by sympathy for the rough-hewn boy. He was obviously slow, possibly retarded. Her parents had taught her to be tolerant of less fortunate people.

"Uh, that's good," Laura replied.

Her father snapped over her shoulder, "Don't talk to him."

But Jacob took another step and this time her father backpedaled. "I got me two brothers," he went on. "They ain't much for workin' like me and Paw. Boy, you sure are purty, miss."

Mr. Hollister jerked forward, positioning himself between Laura and the boy. "Look here, you can't talk to her like that! Somebody should teach you some manners."

Jacob's face contorted into an animalistic expression. "Cain't nobody talk to *me* like that! You're the one who needs manners."

Laura was going to say something to mediate the argument, but she caught movement out of the corner of her eye. The grubby father had come back around the side of the truck, sidling over slowly with something in his hand. It looked like an ax handle or a baseball bat. The weapon hung from his right hand, half hidden behind his leg. His face had also grown tense with anger.

"Dad," Laura said nervously, "let's just go."

"Don't you like me?" Jacob asked.

The ugly father kept coming, almost on tiptoes, stalking his prey.

Mr. Hollister had begun to sense that the other man might get violent. "Er, okay, Laura— yes, you're right."

Mrs. Hollister had climbed out of the station wagon. "Jim! Jim, what's wrong?"

Jacob's eyes had gotten softer, almost moony. "You shore are purty," he said again to Laura.

But Laura was watching the boy's father. The weapon, definitely an ax handle, had come into full view. The filthy man's dark expression told her that he intended to use the club against her father.

"Dad!"

Mr. Hollister was starting to back off when they heard the sudden blast of a police siren. Flashing blue lights threw an eerie sheen on the faces of the junk-men. A state trooper pulled around the truck, stopping behind the two men. The boy's father immediately threw the club to the ground.

"Thank God," Laura said aloud.

But then a frightening thought hit her. What if the trooper is with *them*?

The state policeman got out of the cruiser, sauntering toward the scene of the accident. He surveyed the road with steely blue eyes. With his hands on his hips, he walked around the truck first, then the Hollister's car. Snowflakes dropped on his wide-brimmed gray hat.

As he sauntered toward them again, Laura became aware that the trooper had rested his hand on the butt of a large pistol that hung at his side. "I'm Officer Royer. Anybody want to tell me what happened?"

Mr. Hollister, whose irate demeanor had returned, spoke first. "These two pulled out in front of me."

"You were driving?" the trooper asked.

"Er, no, it was my wife . . . she—"

Officer Royer waved him off, glancing toward the father. "Caleb. How you been? I see you're still selling used furniture."

Laura's heart skipped a beat. They did know each other. What would that mean to a family who were strangers to the area?

Jacob spoke for his father. "We was pullin' off the road, Mr. Royer. Then this car screeches behind us. We didn't even see it. Just came up on us real quick. Slid off that way."

"But you did pull out?" the officer asked.

Jacob hung his head. "Yes sir."

The officer sighed. "Anybody hurt?"

Mr. Hollister shook his head. "No, but this man was coming after me with that stick."

The steely eyes glanced at the ax handle on the ground. "That so, Caleb?"

"No. I was gonna help 'em get their car out of that ditch. Thought I might need somethin' to dig with. I don't have no shovel."

Laura's father opened his mouth to say something hostile, but Laura pinched him. "It's okay, sir. Nobody's hurt," she said quickly.

"You want to bring any charges?" the trooper asked.

"Er, no," Mr. Hollister replied. "But I think an apology would be in order."

The boy's father quickly removed his orange

hat, revealing a crusted, balding scalp. "I sure am sorry about this, sir."

The trooper started toward the wagon. "Come on, let's see if we can get you back on the road."

Laura was relieved as the tension began to ease. With the help of the trooper and the two local men, the back wheel of the family car was quickly freed from the ditch. Laura was aware of the young boy's eyes that never seemed to leave her. He appeared to believe that Laura liked him, though she did not cast even one glance in his direction.

When the station wagon was back on the shoulder of the road, the trooper asked to see Mrs. Hollister's driver's license. He also asked for the license of the boy. But he didn't write any tickets.

"No harm done," he said to them. "Where would you folks be heading, Mr. Hollister?"

"A place called Cook's Cabin," Laura's father replied.

Laura cringed when she saw the boy and his father exchange another look. They seemed to recognize the name. Great, she thought, now they know where we're staying.

The trooper glanced at father and son. "Caleb, you and your boy get on with your business, otherwise I'll have to ticket you for that expired inspection sticker on your truck. You better have it inspected the next time I see you."

"Yes sir," the dirty man said.

Jacob cast one last look at Laura. "Good-bye, miss. Hope to see you again."

I hope not, Laura thought fervently.

The trooper remained silent until the men had driven off in the junk-truck.

"You're a long way from home," he said to Mr. Hollister.

Laura's father was gazing at the disappearing shape of the junk-truck. "Er, yes, we plan to spend two weeks up here."

Officer Royer gave them a reassuring smile. "Don't worry about Caleb and his son. They're harmless."

"He was really coming after me with that stick," Mr. Hollister insisted.

The trooper shook his head. "I doubt it. Caleb doesn't want any trouble with the law. There's still a few men like him up this way. Backwoods types. Just stay out of their way and they'll leave you alone."

Mrs. Hollister, who was still a little shaken, touched her husband's arm. "Jim, let's get up to the lake. It's going to be dark soon."

Officer Royer gave a little laugh. "Cook's Cabin isn't on the lake, ma'am. It's on Indian Pond. I know the place. Would you like me to escort you there?"

Laura was happy to have the policeman show them the way to the cottage. As the sky grew darker overhead, they followed the taillights of the patrol car, winding through what seemed to be endless miles of slick, narrow roads. Laura half expected the junk-truck to pull out in front of them again, but there was no sign of the creepy father-son team. She shivered every time she thought of the way the boy had leered at her, like a wolf eyeing a succulent lamb.

She became nervous again when the trooper went off the road, driving back into a thicket of trees. The station wagon bounced on a snow-covered dirt trail that was barely wide enough for the cars to pass through. Twigs scraped the glass of the windows, frightening Amy and making Laura a little uneasy. She hadn't expected the place to be this far back in the forest. Maybe running away wasn't such a hot idea.

The trooper's car burst into a clearing. Mr. Hollister followed him. Laura could see the cabin above them at the top of a gradual incline. The trooper turned around in the clearing and waved to them, heading off back toward the main road. Laura was sorry to see him go. Now they were alone in the wilderness.

Mr. Hollister pulled up next to the dark cabin. "Everyone out. We finally made it."

Mrs. Hollister gazed at the cabin. "It's awfully dark."

Mr. Hollister shrugged. "I'll go in and turn on the lights."

Laura held her breath as she watched her father get out of the car and trudge into the cabin. She let it out when the lights came on. Mr. Hollister rushed outside, urging them to join him.

"It's great," he said excitedly. "The place is beautiful. And Mr. Cook left us some food. Come on."

Mrs. Hollister said she was tired and didn't want to unpack until morning. So they all went into the cabin without any luggage. It was nice, Laura thought, rustic wood and a big fireplace. The kids would have private bedrooms. Too bad she wouldn't be staying.

To put on a front, she helped her mother make sandwiches. Junior and Amy plopped down in front of a color television set. Mr. Hollister joined them. Laura played it cool and collected, as if nothing was wrong. She kept watching the clock, hoping she would have enough time to make it to the midnight bus. It was going to be a long walk in the snow.

They ate quickly and by nine-thirty everyone had gone to bed. Laura lay in her own single bunk, looking up at the ceiling. As soon as her father started to snore, she knew she was free.

Rising from the bunk, she began to move through the cabin, tiptoeing in the darkness. Outside, the wind was howling. Even though the calendar said it was spring, Mother Nature wasn't cooperating.

Laura found the front door. When she emerged into the darkness, she felt the cold air on her skin. Flurries of spring snow still filled the air with swirling dots of white. It wasn't exactly the best night for traveling on foot.

Hesitating on the deck of the cabin, she

wondered if perhaps it might be better to delay her departure. After all, the bus came through every night at twelve. But then she thought about Charlie, surrounded by the other girls who wanted to steal him away. She started forward with a new resolve.

Her father had turned off the outside lights, so she had to feel her way along the side of the cabin. The flurries pelted her face with cold specks of snow. Laura stopped for a moment, pulling the drawstring on the hood of her parka so she could shield her face from the wind.

As she moved forward again, leaving the cabin behind, her feet made crunching noises in the snow. The dirt road in front of her was dark and threatening. She tried to remember the twists and turns that would take her back to the main road. It had to be after ten o'clock. She hoped there was enough time to hitchhike to the midnight bus.

She hadn't walked far on the road when the wind died suddenly. Laura was thankful, at least until she heard the crashing sound in the woods to her left. She stopped, not sure what she had heard.

More strange noises rose from the thick forest. Something was moving around between the trees. Laura gulped cold air, standing dead still.

It had to be an animal.

Junior's Wendigo teasing rung in her ears. *The Wendigo likes to eat human flesh.* Laura shook off the shudder that played through her spine. There weren't any monsters in the north woods.

She started down the road again.

Her feet crunched in the snow, but there was an even louder rustling that rose over the sound of her footsteps.

The intruder, whatever it was, had begun to move again.

And Laura quickly came to the conclusion that it was following her.

SEVEN

Laura froze on the snow-packed trail. The noise in the woods didn't stop. It kept coming in her direction.

A voice went off in her head, bursting like fireworks. *Go back—now!*

"No," she whispered. "I have to be with Charlie."

Crunching footsteps inched closer to her. The intruder in the woods didn't care if Laura knew it was there. The Wendigo didn't care.

"There's no such thing as a Wendigo," she whispered.

Go back!

But she started toward the main highway anyway.

The intruder got closer picking up speed in the forest. Laura was almost sure that it had passed by her. She tried to walk faster herself, but the Wendigo was more than keeping pace.

Laura felt her body stiffening. She stopped

again on the trail. The crashing in the woods faded from her realm of perception. For a moment, she was blinded by a bright, white-hot light that seemed to appear before her eyes.

Go back before it's too late! the strangely detached voice warned.

The light faded. Laura returned to her senses. She heard the intruder again, moving ahead of her, off to the right, deep in the woods . . .

She flashed on the boy and his father, the men in the orange hunting caps who had almost caused an accident. It was them! They had come to get her.

She remembered the way the boy had looked at her.

You sure are purty, miss.

Laura quickly abandoned her escape plans. She turned back toward the cabin. She had to get to her father. He would protect her from the men.

A roaring filled her head, like the muttering of many voices. She couldn't hear the intruder for a moment. Then, as the voices faded, the rustling noise came back, rising from the woods like a dirge of death.

It seemed to be following her again, reversing direction to come after her. They were going to kidnap her, Laura thought. She was going to be forced to marry the retarded boy. Or maybe something worse.

Given a choice, she would have preferred the Wendigo.

Laura struggled to get back to the cabin. Her legs had grown stiff from the cold. She hadn't noticed the incline of the road until she tried to climb it in the snow. She stumbled, falling on her knees, rising again, and attempting, but failing, to run.

The sound in the woods moved with her, following a parallel path. No matter how fast she ran, the intruder seemed faster. It was going to catch her.

She saw the outline of the cabin ahead of her, a dark shape against the night sky. If she could just make it back to the warmth of the bedroom. . . .

Then a huge shape darted out of the woods, right in front of her.

Laura tripped and fell into the snow. The intruder towered over her. She expected to hear the voices of the boy and his father. Or the howling of the Wendigo. The creature gave a deep grunt as it lowered its head.

"Helllp!" Laura screamed into the night.

The monster's warm breath touched her face.

"Daaad!"

Another roar from the Wendigo.

"Please help me! Somebody!"

The outside lights clicked on at the corners of the cabin. Laura saw the face of her attacker more clearly. She gazed in wide-eyed terror at what looked like an enormous horse-shaped creature with a beard. A bellowing echoed out of the monster's ugly maw.

"Laura!"

Mr. Hollister had burst from the cabin in his robe.

"Dad!"

The creature stood its ground, sounding off again.

"Laura, don't move!"

Mr. Hollister ran toward her, flapping his arms and yelling like a madman. Had he lost his mind? Did he really think he could stand up to this . . . *thing*?

The beast gave another unearthly roar and turned to face her father.

"Get out of here!" Mr. Hollister cried. "Go on, beat it!"

After a final grunt of protest, the Wendigo turned to bound off into the darkness of the forest.

Laura's father knelt next to her. "Honey, are you okay?"

She nodded slowly. "What was it?"

He laughed nervously. "A moose. They'll stand their ground sometimes."

He helped Laura to her feet.

"A moose?" Laura said. "But it was following me."

"They're just curious," her father replied. "What the devil were you doing out here anyway?"

Laura thought she was caught. "Uh, I—I

couldn't sleep, so I came out to the car to get one of my magazines."

Mr. Hollister seemed to buy her excuse. "Come on, you'd better go to bed. It's been a tough day for all of us, but I'm sure things will look brighter in the morning."

He led her back to the cabin. Mrs. Hollister, who had also been awakened, met them in the living room. She wasn't amused by the moose story. She also didn't seem to believe Laura's excuse for being outside.

"You'd better settle down, young lady," she told her daughter.

"I'm sorry," Laura replied.

"Come on," her father said. "Let's all get to bed before we wake up Junior and Amy."

Laura returned to her room and lay back on the bed, still dressed. The moose had shaken her, but when she heard her father snoring again, she began to think about bolting. It was ten forty-five. That gave her an hour and fifteen minutes to get to the bus station.

A voice came into her head for a moment. *You can't leave.*

It was just her fear, she thought, the dread of walking to the bus station on a snowy spring night.

She could still go.

They couldn't stop her.

A moose surely couldn't stop her.

You can't leave.

Outside the windows of the cabin, the wind

began to howl again. Laura thought about Charlie. Was he missing her as much as she missed him? Or was he picking up every single girl in Port City?

I hate them, Laura thought, I hate them for doing this to me. I'm going to show them. I'm going to leave.

But as she lay on the bed, listening to the foreign sounds of the black wilderness, she decided to delay her departure for at least another day, when the next midnight bus came through Greenville.

Laura stood at the edge of Indian Pond, gazing out over the thick, frozen surface of ice. It was a cold, March afternoon, a horrible time for a girl's seventeenth birthday. April was almost here but there was no spring warmth for Laura, no crocus or daffodil to cheer her with a colorful blossom.

The first seven days at Cook's Cabin had been interminable for the pretty girl with the up-turned nose. Her parents had forbidden her to call Charlie, saying that the long distance bills would be too expensive. They were doing everything within their power to keep her away from the boy she loved.

Charlie had written her one letter, telling her how much he missed her. He was so sweet. He couldn't afford to call because he was helping his mother with the rent.

Kimmy, on the other hand, had called every

other day, sometimes talking to Laura for
nearly an hour. She kept Laura informed about
the goings-on in their circle of friends. Accord-
ing to Kimmy, Charlie was being a perfect
gentleman, staying at home when he wasn't
working. He hadn't so much as looked at another girl, though Kimmy seemed to think that
one or two of Port City's more aggressive vixens
had an eye on him.

Kimmy's calls made Laura miss Port City
even more. She wanted to go home on the
midnight bus, something she had intended to
do but had postponed every day since her ar-
rival in this wilderness.

Back in Port City, her friends were having
parties and enjoying themselves. A few of the
lucky ones had even gone south to Florida to
frolic on the beaches of Fort Lauderdale or
Daytona. But poor Laura, who had been acting
really pouty for a whole week, was stuck with a
frozen pond and a pair of rusty ice skates.

The skates dangled from her hand. She had
found them in the closet of her bedroom. She
liked skating and thought it might take her
mind off her sorrows.

She could still leave if she wanted to. She was
seventeen now. She had the right to do whatever she pleased. After all, she would be a
senior next year.

So why couldn't she leave?

She wasn't afraid of walking back to Greenville in the dark. On several occasions, she had

charted the course to the road. She knew from
the odometer on her father's car that it was only
four miles to Greenville on the main highway.
She could walk or run that in time to make it to
the bus.

But the departure hadn't happened. Even
when she would rise from her bed, bag packed
for the journey, something stopped her from
escaping. She would get to the door of the cabin
or the base of the dirt road and then turn
around, the little voice in her head working
overtime.

You can't leave.

What was it?

She loved her family, but that wasn't the real
reason.

And she wanted to be with Charlie, to hang
out with Kimmy.

But she couldn't bring herself to do it, to run
away.

What was stopping her?

"Laura?"

She glanced back over her shoulder, scowling
at her mother who had appeared on the high
porch of the cabin. Laura had walked down a
flight of steps to get to the pond and her mother
had come out to check on her. Her father had
taken the car into Greenville earlier that morning.

"I'm all right, Mom!"

Mrs. Hollister, who had been tolerant of her

daughter's moods, gazed out over the frozen pond. "Are you going skating?"

"Yes!" she replied sulkily.

"Honey, I don't think you should try it. It's awfully late in the year to be out on a pond like this. The ice might be too thin."

Laura sighed defeatedly. "Okay."

But as soon as Mrs. Hollister went back into the house, Laura started to put on the skates. When she had tied the laces, she glided out onto the smooth surface of the pond, wobbling for a few minutes until she found her balance. She had never been a strong skater, but she was good enough to keep from falling down.

She skated toward the middle of the pond, thinking what a beautiful place this was. If only Charlie could have been there with her. They could have had so much fun, cuddling in front of the fireplace and taking long walks in the snow.

The wind whooshed over her cheeks, turning them red. Her blood was flowing with the exercise. She stretched out her arms, gliding close to the opposite bank of the pond, trying to execute a turn.

Laura hit a rough patch of ice and fell, landing with a thud on her backside. She sighed and started to get up. But a sudden feeling of light-headedness stopped her. She sat there until a bright light appeared behind her eyes, dazzling her, blinding her with its mysterious glow.

A voice came into her head: *Don't leave them.*

Then another: *If you leave them, they will die.*

She saw her father and mother, Junior and Amy. They were smiling. And then they turned to skeletons, staring at her with lifeless eyes.

Don't leave them.

If you leave them, they will die.

The glow disappeared from behind her eyes. She stood up, feeling stronger than ever. Her entire body tingled with an electric intensity that was almost pleasurable. There seemed to be no weight to her, no mass, like she was a feather dipping in the cold wind.

"I better get back," she said to herself.

But as she turned toward the cabin, her dark eyes focused on the bare trees that ringed the entire pond. Something flashed between the tree trunks. At first Laura thought it was a red winter bird flitting from naked branch to evergreen bough. But it wasn't a bird.

The hue was bright orange, the color of a hunting cap.

Laura gaped at the flash of a white face that peeked out at her. The orange cap seemed to be coming toward her. Was it that weird boy from the highway and the junk-truck? She didn't want to wait around to find out.

As she turned, she heard the thin patch of ice giving way. Suddenly the surface of the pond broke, dropping her into the frigid water. Fortunately, she was in the shallows, so she only sank up to her knees. But she could hear the boy in the orange hunting cap as he moved toward her through the woods.

She had to get away.

He was almost on her.

Had he been watching her all along?

What if his father had come with him?

Laura fell forward on the ice, crawling out of the hole. She slid on her stomach until she was in the middle of the pond. Standing again, she glanced over her shoulder one last time to see the boy coming out of the woods to the edge of the pond. It *was* him. He gawked at her with that moony expression on his dumb face.

With a sudden burst of energy born of fear, Laura began to skate away from the boy. She lost her balance once, sprawling on the ice. But it held and she did not go into the water this time. When she rose, she looked back, wondering if the boy had a pair of skates so he could follow her. But he was no longer standing at the edge of the pond. He had reentered the woods, the orange cap disappearing behind a snow-laden evergreen.

Laura skated back toward the cabin, wishing that they weren't so isolated from the rest of the world. Cook's place was the only house on the pond. If the two horrid men from the junk-truck came back, Laura's family was all alone.

Don't leave them.

If you leave them, they will die.

When she reached the bank of the pond below the cabin, she looked up and called, "Mom!"

Her lonely echo was the only reply. Why couldn't her mother hear her? Sound carried in the wilderness. Her mother had called from the cabin many times and Laura had been able to hear her.

"Dad!"

Where had everyone gone? Laura took off the skates and found her snow boots. Her legs were freezing from the fall through the ice.

"Mom? Dad?"

As she bounced up the wooden steps, she saw that the curtains had been drawn over the glass doors. Hesitating on the stairs, she called again but no one answered. Surely they could hear her. But the storm shutters had been closed. She wondered if her father had come back from Greenville yet.

Laura eased onto the porch, moving to the side of the cabin, peering toward the station wagon. The car was there, parked in the usual spot. What if the two men from the junk-truck had come back? No, it was too far for the strange boy to make it all the way around the pond on foot. But did it matter? Couldn't the crazy father do enough harm by himself?

Don't leave them.

If you leave them, they will die.

The words spun inside her skull like a fever.

She wanted to run.

No, if there was someone inside the cabin, he knew she was there. Surely he had heard her calling for her family. If she ran, wouldn't he come after her?

She had to look inside.

What if they were all lying in there dead?

The wind started to pick up, freezing her. "Dad?"

She remembered the spectral light that had visited her twice.

If you leave them, they will die.

Sliding around the house to the glass doors in back, Laura listened for signs of life.

What if the crazy father killed them and then left?

Laura shook her head, wondering how she could have such thoughts. What had crawled into her brain to raise these horrible images? She saw her family lying on the floor in a pool of half-dried blood.

Don't leave them.

She couldn't stand the cold much longer, not with her legs frozen. She had to go inside to get warm. Her hand reached for the glass door.

Laura pushed firmly and cautiously entered the dim cabin.

EIGHT

The inside of the cabin was bathed in shadows. The storm shutters blocked out the light. Laura hesitated in the doorway, peering into the darkness. Where were they? What had happened to her family?

"Mom?"

Her voice came out as a timid squeak. A snake had wrapped itself around her windpipe, constricting her throat. Something had happened. She was sure of it.

"Dad?"

A bright light flashed again, only this time it was directly hitting her eyes. Laura reached up to cover her face. She heard movement in the cabin. Someone was coming toward her in the wake of the blinding light.

Laura tried to retreat. "No!"

She felt a hand on her arm, grabbing her.

"Surprise!"

They were all around her, pulling her into the cabin.

"Happy Birthday, Laura!"

She opened her eyes.

"Happy Birthday," Junior said. "Let's have some cake!"

Laura was still trembling even after she realized what had happened. Her family had surrounded her for a surprise party. It was almost as great a shock as falling through the ice and seeing the boy in the orange hunting cap.

Amy kissed her on the cheek. "Happy Birthday, sis."

Her mother carried a cake that blazed with seventeen candles. "I baked a coconut cake, your favorite, honey."

Mr. Hollister pointed to the pile of brightly wrapped birthday gifts in front of the fireplace. "Happy seventeenth, princess."

Laura was speechless. So much had happened so fast. She hadn't been expecting all this kindness from her family, not after the way she had been sulking for a week.

A surge of emotion welled inside her. She fought back the tears but they were almost ready to cascade down her cheeks.

"Guess what?" he said with a wide grin on his face. "I have another birthday present for you. Ta-da!"

The door to Laura's bedroom swung open.

She saw the petite blond girl standing in the doorway. Laura couldn't believe it.

"Only seventeen, Hollister? You look so much older!"

"Kimmy!" Laura cried. "How . . ."

Kimmy came toward her. "Your mom and dad paid for my bus ticket up here. They didn't want me to miss your birthday."

Laura rushed toward Kimmy, wrapping her arms around her best friend. Everyone thought she was shedding tears of joy. And Laura was in no shape to tell them they were tears of fear.

Mrs. Hollister gawked at Laura's wet legs. "What happened?"

Laura could not reply because she was so choked with emotion.

Mrs. Hollister's face turned red. "I told you not to skate on the pond. You could have been—"

Mr. Hollister put his arm around his wife's shoulder. "Take it easy, honey. It's her birthday."

Laura just clung to Kimmy, thinking that it felt really good to cry.

Laura sat in front of the fireplace with warm socks covering her feet. The birthday gifts lay unwrapped around her chair. Mr. Hollister had given her a colorful designer watch. Her mother had come through with a new book bag. Junior had given her a crudely made birthday card, complete with a smudge of peanut butter. A coupon for two dollars off a large pizza at the Pizza Barn had been Amy's offering.

Laura sighed. "It's all so great. Especially having Kimmy here. I—I don't know what to say."

Kimmy stood up quickly. "Wait, you haven't opened my present yet." She ran into Laura's bedroom.

"I thought her just being here was my present," Laura said.

"That's from us," her father replied.

Junior thrust his plate at Mrs. Hollister. "Can I have some more cake?"

Amy grimaced. "You're such a little piggy."

"Oink, oink," Junior mocked. "I'm going to sic the Wendigo on you!"

Laura shuddered, feeling the cold in her whole body. For a moment, she remembered the strange boy standing at the edge of the pond, gawking at her with his expectant face, and the voices in her head. . . .

Kimmy came rushing back in the living room to dispel the horrid mood. "I couldn't think of what to get you. So I got creative. Here, I hope you like it." She thrust a large box toward Laura.

Laura liked the shiny red foil paper. "It's beautiful."

"Well, open it!" Kimmy insisted.

Laura ripped the paper, revealing the color-ful imprint on the box. "A Ouija board?"

Kimmy lifted her hands in the air, wiggling her fingers and talking in a spooky voice. "Reveals all. Know the secret mysteries of the universe. Talk to spirits from beyond the grave."

Amy moved closer to her mother. "She's scaring me!"

Junior looked at the box. "Neat!"

"It's just a game," Kimmy insisted. "I'm sorry, Mrs. Hollister, I didn't mean to scare Amy."

Mrs. Hollister stroked her younger daughter's head. "It's alright, Kimmy. I think Amy needs to read in her room for a while. Come on, honey." She led Amy out of the living room.

Mr. Hollister stood up. "Well, I have some work to do. I'll leave you girls to ice out."

Laura made a face. "It's chill out, Dad!"

Kimmy laughed. "Nice try, Mr. Hollister."

Junior tried to grab the Ouija board from Laura's hand. "Let's call somebody from the grave."

Laura drew back. "You're going to the grave if you don't chill out, you little dweeb."

"I wanna play!" Junior whined.

Mr. Hollister motioned to his son. "Come on, Junior. Kimmy and Laura have a lot of catching up to do." He exited, dragging a disappointed Junior with him.

Laura looked at Kimmy and sighed. She wondered if she should tell Kimmy about what had happened on the pond. She decided to keep the bizarre experience to herself. It must have been some sort of hallucination brought on by the cold. And the boy in the hunting cap had probably been doing some backwoods stuff that led him to stumble onto Laura by accident. Everything was going to be all right.

Kimmy squinted cautiously at her. "Everything okay?"

Laura nodded. "I guess."

"You look like you've seen a ghost."

Laura thought she was going to cry again, but she managed to hold back the tears this time. "It's been *sooo* boring here."

"I can imagine," Kimmy replied. "When your mom called me, I jumped at the chance to come. It's really pretty up here."

Laura leaned closer, whispering, "I was going to run away. But I kept chickening out."

"It's only a few more days," Kimmy replied. "Hang in there. Charlie is dying to see you. He can't stand it."

"Neither can I. Is he all right?"

Kimmy curled her upper lip. "Brenda Jordan has been calling him all the time, trying to get him to go out with her. But Charlie blows her off."

Laura's face turned red. "That flirt! I'm going to scratch her eyes out when I get back to Port City."

Kimmy waved at her. "Don't worry. She's stupid, even if she call fill out a sweater. Charlie hates her."

"So do I."

Laura was seized by a sudden urge to call
Charlie. She wanted to hear his voice and tell
him how much she loved him.

"Are you sure you're all right?" Kimmy asked
in a tone of genuine concern.

"I don't know. This place is just so . . .
creepy. That's the only word I have for it."

"It's not that bad," Kimmy said. "Although
I'm not so sure I'd want to be stuck here for two
weeks with *my* mom."

Laura gave a nervous laugh. "Try being stuck
here with Junior. I swear, I think he sleeps in a
coffin."

Kimmy started to laugh. "You crack me up."

In a few moments, they were both laughing
uncontrollably. Laura felt a lot better having
Kimmy around. Kimmy reminded her of all the
good stuff back in Port City.

Kimmy grabbed the box that contained the
Ouija board. "Come on, let's play."

Laura grimaced. "Are you sure about this?"

"It looks like fun," Kimmy replied. "I used to
have one when I was a kid. You just ask it
questions and it tells you the answers."

"I don't know—"

"It'll be fun, Laura."

They sat knee to knee in two dining room
chairs, holding the board between them.
Kimmy took out the triangular-shaped
planchette that was supposed to move back and
forth on the board. The writing on the board

contained numbers, the letters of the alphabet, and YES and NO, all written in spooky script.

Kimmy put her hands on one side of the triangular piece. "Come on, put your hands here."

Laura placed her hands on the triangular piece. When her fingertips touched the Ouija board, she felt a little shock. She drew back immediately.

Kimmy frowned at her. "What?"

Laura shrugged. "I don't know. I just felt something."

"Probably static electricity," Kimmy replied. "Try it again."

Laura cautiously put her fingertips on the board. She didn't feel the shock this time. She thought it was kind of stupid, nothing but a parlor game.

"Kimmy—"

"Shh! Let's ask it a question."

Laura sighed. "Okay." She knew when Kimmy got something in her mind, it was hard to stop her from obsessing.

Kimmy closed her eyes. "Will Laura and Charlie get married?"

Laura grimaced and rolled her eyes.

But suddenly, the planchette started to move. The triangle slid across the board, stopping at the word YES. Laura wasn't buying it.

"Kimmy! You pushed that over to the YES."

Kimmy opened her eyes. "Gotcha!"

Laura pulled her hands away from the board. "This is dumb."

"No," Kimmy insisted. "Keep going."

Laura shook her head. "What's the point?"

"To know the future."

"Who wants to—"

For a moment Laura saw the bright light again. It seemed to burn behind her eyes, like before on the pond. When it faded, she glanced down to see that she had her fingers on the board again.

"Great," Kimmy said. "Let's play."

Laura hesitated. "I—"

But Kimmy went ahead and asked the next question. "How many children will Laura and Charlie have?"

The planchette didn't move.

Kimmy shrugged. "Okay. Let me ask for real this time. Oh spirits of the great beyond—" she intoned.

"Kimmy, shut up."

"We summon you to answer this question for us. Will Charlie and Laura ever get married?"

The triangular piece remained stationary, unmoved by the spirits of the great beyond.

"I told you it was stupid," Laura insisted.

"Then you ask a question."

Laura shuddered. A coldness had overtaken her body. For a moment, her eyes were drawn to the fireplace. She saw unreal shapes in the flames, lost, tortured souls who writhed in torment in a dance of the damned.

The light returned, this time brighter than ever. She wasn't aware of anything except the eerie glow. There was a peace in it, but she sensed danger too. Where had the light come from?

Kimmy's voice faded in suddenly. "Oh, that's nice."

Laura's head snapped to one side. She gazed into Kimmy's smiling face. Kimmy seemed to be happy about something.

"That's really nice, Laura. Thanks."

Laura was cold again. "Nice?"

"What you spelled on the board."

Laura looked down at the Ouija board. The planchette was resting on the letter "E." But Laura wasn't aware of spelling anything. She had been taken away by the weird light.

"I'm glad I have you for a best friend," Kimmy went on. "But don't worry, everything will be all right."

Laura still didn't get it. "What are you talking about?"

"Look, it's not so bad up here," Kimmy replied. "And I have to go back on the midnight bus. Mom is expecting me. She'd have a fit if I wasn't there in the morning. But that was nice."

Laura's eyes were fixed on the board. "Kimmy, what did it spell out?"

Kimmy hesitated for a moment, staring into Laura's glassy eyes. "Are you okay, Laura?"

"Yes, just tell me what the board spelled."

Kimmy touched her throat. "This isn't funny, Laura. Don't try to frighten me like this."

Laura attempted to laugh and remain calm, even though she was scared and confused on the inside. "Kimmy, I wasn't looking when I spelled it. I just want to make sure it came out right."

Kimmy relaxed a little. "Oh. Well, you were just great. You spelled it perfectly."

"Really are you sure?"

"Uh-huh. It was plain as day. 'You can't leave.' But I have to—"

Laura faded again. She hadn't spelled out the words, not consciously anyway. As Kimmy chattered on, Laura heard the voices again in her head.

If you leave, they'll die.

What was happening to her?

She was blacking out, having visions in her head, hearing things, seeing the bizarre light. She had spelled something on the board. No, she hadn't—something else had done it.

Kimmy's voice came back. "—And then we all went for pizza. They really miss you, Laura."

Laura nodded, not wanting to seem weird. In her mind, she was going over the possibilities, trying to explain what was happening to her. Maybe she was losing her grip on reality, slipping into madness. Sometimes brain tumors could cause such problems; she had seen it on television in a rerun episode of an old doctor show. Something bad was going on inside her head.

"Laura, honey."

She looked up to see her mother standing at the entrance to the kitchen.

"Yes?"

"You want to help me get dinner started?" Mrs. Hollister asked.

Kimmy stood up quickly. "I'll help, Mrs. H. Let the birthday girl take it easy."

When Kimmy went into the kitchen with Laura's mother, Laura turned her eyes to the board again. Maybe someone or some *thing* was attempting to contact her from the spirit world. She decided to try one more time.

With her fingertips on the planchette she asked the one question that had begun to burn in her mind. "Will those men with the hunting caps hurt us?"

But there was no response from the Ouija board.

The spirits of the netherworld had suddenly grown quiet.

NINE

The north wind howled outside the cabin, sweeping through the forest like an evil force from a Scandinavian fairy tale. Earlier in the evening, just after Laura's experience with the Ouija board, Mr. Hollister had checked the wooden storm shutters that sealed them away from the raging gale. He had made a funny remark about the way early settlers had protected themselves from hostile elements by shutting up their cabins.

As it grew later, Junior and Amy were sent to bed. Mr. Hollister also retired at ten-thirty, leaving Laura and Kimmy alone in front of the fire while Mrs. Hollister finished cleaning the rest of the party clutter. Laura was distant, lost in thoughts of an otherworldly nature. She stared into the fire, wondering again what was happening to her. She kept waiting for something else, some sign that she was indeed losing her mind. But nothing came, no flashes of light, no blackouts. She was normal again, even if she didn't really feel that way.

"Are you okay?" Kimmy asked.

Laura nodded, not sure how much of the weirdness she should share with her best friend. Kimmy might not understand it. Why should she? Laura had no idea what was going on herself.

"I better be leaving soon," Kimmy went on. "There's only the one bus out of here tonight. I have to change buses in Lewiston, too."

Laura felt uneasy about Kimmy traveling so late. "Can't you stay tonight? There's an extra bunk in my room."

Kimmy sighed. "I wish I could. Mom wants me back by tomorrow. I can sleep on the bus. It won't be too bad."

Laura lifted her eyes to the clock. It was almost eleven. Kimmy had to be under way before too long.

"Mom," she called into the kitchen, "are you going to take Kimmy to the bus? She has to go soon."

Mrs. Hollister appeared in the living room, frowning. "Laura, could you take her to the bus? I'm awfully tired."

Laura shrugged. "Sure, Mom."

"You two better get going," Mrs. Hollister said. "And you come straight back here, Laura. Okay?"

"Mom! I'm seventeen now. I've been driving for over a year. I can take her to the bus."

"Okay, honey. Just be careful."

"Cool," Kimmy said. "We can talk some more on the way."

As they gathered up Kimmy's coat and purse, another strange feeling came upon Laura. A sense of anticipation had overtaken her, as if she was waiting for something to happen.

Kimmy slipped into her coat. "Ready."

Mrs. Hollister handed Laura the keys to the station wagon. "You make sure you wait until Kimmy is on the bus before you leave."

Laura snatched the keys from her mother's hand. "Oh, like I was going to make her stand out in the cold."

Mrs. Hollister grimaced. "I don't care if you are seventeen now, don't take that tone with me, young lady."

Kimmy cringed, embarrassed by the same kind of interaction that often took place between her and her own mother. "Uh, bye, Mrs. H. Thanks for a nice time. Say bye to Mr. Hollister for me."

Mrs. Hollister ignored Kimmy's polite speech. "You'd better be back no later than twelve-thirty."

Laura started to say something about the possibility of the bus being late. But the words would not come out of her mouth. She felt teary-eyed all of a sudden. The ethereal light glowed for a moment, obscuring her vision.

She heard the words, a whisper in her mind. *If you leave they will die.*

"Do you understand?" her mother asked.

Laura embraced Mrs. Hollister, hugging her tightly. "I love you, Mom. Thanks for everything." She kissed her mother on the cheek.

Mrs. Hollister seemed stunned. "My goodness, what did I do to deserve that? Are you all right, Laura?"

No, Laura thought, hysterically, not really.

Kimmy was gazing at the clock. "We'd better go."

But Laura didn't want to go. She had to stay with her family. The sense of anticipation would not leave her.

"Hurry," her mother urged. "But don't hurry too much when you get on the road. There might be some black ice around."

Black ice referred to the patches of frozen water that collected on the highway when the road was wet and the temperature dropped below freezing.

Kimmy tugged at Laura's arm. "Come on." She had something else for Laura, something she couldn't give her in the midst of the family scene.

Laura hesitated, looking around the cabin. Her family seemed safe enough. The shutters were drawn and there was a good lock on the door. She thought about the boy in the orange hunting cap. Surely he had gone back to his home by now. He couldn't pose a threat to her family, not on such a horrid night.

The wind rattled the shutters.

You can't leave.

If you leave them, they will die.

Her mother frowned at her. "Laura, maybe I had better take Kimmy to the bus. You look like you're coming down with something." She pressed her hand to Laura's forehead, feeling for a fever.

Laura snapped back to her old self. "I'm okay, Mom. I'll hurry back as soon as Kimmy is on the bus."

Kimmy pulled her toward the door and whispered, "Let's go. I have something else for you. And you're going to love it."

Laura slipped on her red parka, following Kimmy into the cold night. The wind bit at their faces, refusing to give in to the influence of spring. Boughs cracked in the high timber of the forest, snapping like bones in the unrelenting darkness. Laura and Kimmy fought their way to the station wagon.

They climbed in, escaping from the wind. Laura put the key in the ignition. The Chevy chugged to life, stalling a few times as it warmed up.

Laura finally put the car in gear, turning in a circle to head down the dirt road. "How'd you get up here anyway?" she asked Kimmy. "I mean, there's only that one bus."

"Your father drove down to Guilford to get me," Kimmy replied. "He even paid for my ticket."

"He's great," Laura admitted. "I had no idea you were coming."

"I took the bus from Port City to Guilford early this morning," Kimmy went on. "We got back while you were ice-skating on the pond."

Laura flashed back again on her strange experiences. She wanted to tell Kimmy. She had to share it with someone, and who better than her best friend? Kimmy would understand.

Kimmy started to dig into her purse. "Listen, I've got something for you."

Laura saw the end of the dirt road ahead of them. She stopped, looked both ways and then pulled out onto the dark highway. She was trying to find the right words to describe what she was feeling.

"Kimmy, I think I'm going crazy."

Kimmy pulled an envelope from her purse. "Well, you're going to go nuts when you read this."

Laura glanced over at her best friend. "What's that?"

"A letter from Charlie."

Laura tensed. Could this letter be the bad news she had been waiting for, the cause of all her apprehension?

"He's breaking up with me, isn't he?" she said to Kimmy.

Kimmy shrugged. "I haven't read the letter, but I doubt it."

"Open it and read it to me," Laura said quickly.

Kimmy hesitated. "I don't know—"

The station wagon barreled along the blacktop, picking up speed as Laura pressed the accelerator. She was going sixty now, flying toward Greenville. She couldn't shake the hateful feeling. Maybe the letter would make it go away.

"Read it," she insisted.

Kimmy opened the letter. "I can't see. Turn on the overhead light."

Laura switched on the dome light so Kimmy could read. Kimmy's eyes began to move over the page. She smiled broadly.

Laura grimaced. "Read it out loud, doofus!"

Kimmy couldn't stop grinning. "Oh, this is great. Listen: 'My dearest Laura, I miss you so much. Kimmy probably told you by now that some other girls have been calling me. I told her to give this to you at the last minute. I can only say that I don't even look at those others. And if I did, I'd only see your face.' Oh, he's dreamy."

Laura had to admit that she liked what she heard. "Is there more?"

"Lots."

"Read on then!"

Kimmy put some emotion into it as the car drew closer to Greenville. "He really loves you, Laura. 'The ring is a symbol of our love. Our complete devotion to each other. I can't live without you, Laura. These days have been unbearable. Hurry back to me. I want to share *everything* with you. I want our love to be complete, our commitment to be total. I hope you feel the same way. It's time we realized that we shouldn't hold back any longer. If we truly love each other, then everything will be perfect. Love, Charlie.' Oh, Laura, why can't someone write me a letter like that?"

Laura eased back on the gas pedal. "Someone will," she replied, half in a dream state. "Gosh, I wasn't ready for this."

"Oooh, there's a P.S.," Kimmy said. "It's great. 'Laura, I'm so sorry that I missed your birthday, but my gift is my love and the ring on your finger. I hope it's enough.' Way cool!"

It is enough, Laura thought.

Kimmy touched her arm. "Laura, come back to Port City with me. You can leave the car at the bus station."

Laura was tempted for a moment.

Kimmy had grown excited by the prospect of an intrigue. "You can dump the car at the bus stop. They'll find it. Think of how great it will be to see Charlie. He'll be so surprised."

Laura imagined Charlie's smile, felt his lips against hers.

"Your mom and dad won't kill you," Kimmy said, egging her on. "They'll be mad for a while and you'll get grounded. But that's about it."

Laura gazed forward into the shadows of the highway. She had planned all along to run away. But the eerie workings of her mind had stopped her. The light flashed for a moment, blinding her.

Laura's stomach quivered as the car hit a dip in the road. She kept her foot off the brake. Her hands clutched the cold steering wheel. When she looked forward again, she saw the Greenville store in the distance.

Kimmy glanced sideways at her. "Laura, are you all right?"

"Kimmy, I think I'm losing my mind."

Kimmy laughed. "Who wouldn't lose it up here? I don't know how you stood it this long."

"No, I mean it."

Kimmy seemed to miss the point. "So, are you coming back to Port City with me? I have some money if you need a ticket."

Laura heard the voice in her head, loud and clear, like a dull roar.

If you leave them, they will die.

She remembered the message spelled out on the Ouija board. She hadn't been aware of her hands moving at the time. The blackout and the weird light had filled her head. What was happening to her?

"I can't go, Kimmy. Not now."

Kimmy sighed. "I guess not. It's just hard to think of Charlie all lonely like that."

"Tell me about it."

But her thoughts weren't really on Charlie. She kept seeing the orange hat in the woods, framed against the snow, and the planchette moving on the Ouija board, telling her not to go.

I hope I am losing my mind, she thought. That would be better than this feeling of something terrible happening.

"Kimmy, there's something strange going on in my head. I don't know what it is. I think there's something wrong with me."

"Oh, you just miss Charlie."

"No, I think it's more than that."

Kimmy shrugged. "Don't worry, you'll be home in a few days. Then you can forget about this place forever."

"I hope so."

You can't leave.

What was the Ouija board trying to tell her?

It was all in her head. It had to be. There was no such thing as ghosts and goblins. Departed spirits didn't visit the living, did they?

"There's the store," Kimmy told her.

Laura pulled into the empty parking lot. They got out and went into the store, which was still open. The old man behind the counter watched them as they grabbed fruit drinks from the cooler.

They stood next to the window, gazing out at the bleak night. Flurries had begun to fall. The snow wasn't sticking though.

Kimmy pulled her coat collar tightly around her neck. "Kind of a lousy night for traveling."

Laura looked back at the old man. "Is the bus running tonight?"

"Far as I know," he replied.

Laura curled her lip. "What he knows could fill up a thimble."

Kimmy rolled her eyes. "Shh. You don't want to provoke the locals. They might—"

The light came and went for a moment. Laura didn't hear what Kimmy was saying. When she refocused, she thought to herself that it must be a brain tumor. Or something just as bad.

Kimmy chattered on as midnight approached. Laura stood there beside her best friend, gazing into the windy darkness. She knew she had to do something about her condition. First off, she would tell her parents. They could get her to a doctor.

You can't leave.

"Oh, shut up!" Laura snapped.

She turned to see Kimmy gaping at her.

"What was that for?" Kimmy asked dumbfoundedly.

Laura shook her head. "I—I don't know."

"Are you really losing it?" Kimmy wondered aloud.

"Yes, I think I am."

But Laura couldn't tell her that she was hearing voices in her head.

Kimmy sighed. "I guess I'd go crazy if I lived up here."

"Kimmy, I—" How could she tell her? "Kimmy, I think there might be something—"

"Oh, look," Kimmy interrupted. "Here's the bus."

Laura saw the bright glare of the motor coach. For a moment, she thought she was seeing the lights in her head again. But then the coach turned and she was no longer blinded.

Kimmy gave her a hug. "What do you want me to tell Charlie?"

Laura hesitated. She should have written Charlie a letter for hand delivery. But everything had happened so quickly, the pond, the birthday party, and now the midnight bus. She thought about going with Kimmy but the voice came into her head, telling her not to leave.

"Just tell him I love him," Laura replied.

Kimmy squeezed her hand. "Sure. C'mon, walk me out."

As they exited, the old man locked the front door and went to his own car, ending his day.

Laura watched as Kimmy boarded the bus and paid for her ticket. When Kimmy had taken her seat, Laura waved and smiled. Maybe things weren't that bad after all. She'd be home soon, like Kimmy, back to her life in Port City.

The bus rumbled and then pulled away from the Greenville Corner Market. Laura shivered in the cold. She had to get back to the cabin. Some unknown force drew her back toward the station wagon.

She climbed behind the wheel and started to turn the key. But the key wasn't there. She patted the pockets of her coat but she didn't hear any jingling.

"Darn it."

She figured she had dropped the keys in the parking lot. Or even worse, in the locked store. She had to get out and look for them.

As she opened the car door again, she heard the jingling sound.

"Lookin' for these?"

The voice had come from the shadows behind the store. Laura froze when the dark figure stepped out with the keys dangling from his fingers. Even in the black of night, she could tell that he wore a bright orange hunting cap.

TEN

Laura recognized the boy's voice. He moved toward her, holding the keys in front of him. But when Laura tried to take them out of his hand, he pulled them back. She knew she had to flee.

"You sure are purty, miss."

Laura wheeled away from him, running toward the highway. She saw the lights again. This time, they came from the junk-truck that pulled in front of her, blocking her path. The boy's father and two other men jumped out of the truck, stopping Laura.

The father leered at her. "You think you're too good for my boy, city girl?"

Laura tried to bolt, rushing back in the direction of the store. The boy was there in front of her. Three other hunting caps circled around her.

The father's voice rose over the wind. "You're

gonna marry my boy, city girl. I ain't gonna talk to your father about it."

Laura stood there, surrounded by her assailants, unable to speak. The cold air burned her lungs. Her arms and legs had turned to stone. They were going to haul her away to their— their lair. They were going to make her cook and clean and do unspeakable things.

"Get in the truck," the father said.

The boy stepped up next to Laura, putting his hand on her shoulder. "Aw, don't be mean to her, Paw."

"You shut your mouth, Jacob," the older man snapped.

The other two were closing in on Laura. They had to be Jacob's brothers. What did they have in mind for her?

"She is a looker," one of them said. "Ain't she a looker, Luke?"

The other one laughed. "Maybe *you* ought to marry her, Esau."

"Hush," the father insisted. "Go on, girly. Get in the truck."

Laura stiffened in the wind. The lights had come on in her head again. She waited for the voices to follow.

They can't hurt you.

"You can't hurt me," she repeated.

Jacob gazed into her face with his moony expression. "I won't hurt you. I love you. You and me are gonna be married."

You'll never marry him, the voice assured her.

"I'll never marry you," she said in a trance.

The father gestured toward her. "Luke, Esau, put her in the truck. Go on, do what I tell you."

Laura shrugged away from them. "No!"

The brothers hesitated.

"She don't want to go, Paw."

"Yeah, she don't want to go."

The old man sighed disgustedly. "You ain't afraid of a little city girl, are you? Here, I'll do it myself."

Laura cringed as he took a step toward her.

The father's dirty hands reached for her. He was going to kidnap her. They'd take her some place where no one would ever be able to find her.

"No!"

Another barrage of lights blinded her. Only this time it was the glare of a car. A blue flashing light bathed the store with a strobe effect. A highway patrol cruiser had rolled into the parking lot.

Suddenly the father and sons were scattering away from Laura, trying to look nonthreatening as the officer got out of the cruiser. His hand was on the handle of his pistol as he walked toward them. The two brothers, Luke and Esau, retreated quickly to the junk-truck.

"What's going on here?" the patrolman asked.

Laura rushed toward him when she recog-

nized Officer Royer's voice. "They—they were—
I—" She could barely speak.

Jacob took a step toward Officer Royer. "The
girl here lost her keys. We was just helping her
look for them."

"Yeah," the father replied. "That's it."

"No," Laura whimpered. "They were going to
take me with them."

Jacob held out the car keys. "Sorry, miss. I
hope we didn't scare you. I mean, it is late and
all—"

"They were going to kidnap me," Laura went
on. "They were going to make me marry him!"

The father laughed. "Ain't no such thing.
Shoot, she just lost her keys."

Officer Royer nodded toward the truck.
"Caleb, take your boys and clear out of here."

"I swear I'm telling the truth," Laura insisted. "They were going to—"

Officer Royer waved his hand. "It's okay,
miss. Jacob, get your father and brothers and
go on home."

"Yes sir."

Laura watched them climb into the truck and
take off, heading in the direction of Indian
Pond. The red lights of their junk-truck turned
the corner and disappeared. The voices had
been right—they hadn't hurt her.

"I'm telling the truth," Laura said to the
officer.

He just laughed. "They're country boys, miss.

Mountain men, woodsmen. They have a funny sense of humor."

"But they were going to make me marry that young one."

"No, miss, they wouldn't hurt you. Come on, I'll see to it that you get home all right. I'll follow you back to your cabin."

Go with him, a voice echoed in her head.

Laura returned to the station wagon, putting the key in the ignition. The engine was still warm and turned over easily. In a few minutes, she was heading back to the cabin with Officer Royer behind her. He followed closely with the blue lights going.

Laura took a deep breath, watching for signs of the junk-truck men. The boy *had* been stalking her. He had probably been spying on her the whole time she was at the cabin.

Another voice exploded behind her forehead: *It's not over*.

She saw the turnoff ahead. But when she steered the station wagon onto the dirt road, Officer Royer did not follow her. He only honked the horn and sped off down the highway, disappearing quickly.

Laura guided the station wagon through the trees, emerging in the clearing. Her mother had left the outside light on. Laura easily found her way to the front door of the cabin and entered into the warmth, locking the door behind her. She still didn't feel safe.

She thought about waking her father to tell

him what had happened. But Jim Hollister's snoring filled the night. Laura went into her own bedroom, closing the door. She could tell her parents about it in the morning. If she told them at all. They were leaving soon. Maybe it was better to just forget.

You can't forget.

"Please stop," Laura whispered. "Please get out of my head!"

She fell on the bed, closing her eyes. In a few minutes, a deep sleep came over her. She lay there for a while, lost to the world. Then she began to have a dream. In the dream, the boy was back. He was holding his hand over her mouth, suffocating her, trying to drag her away.

"You're comin' with me, missy."

Laura opened her eyes. The boy stood over her in the shadows, his hand clamped tightly on her mouth. She tried to scream but his palm muffled the desperate cry. Laura felt his breath on her face as he bent down.

This was no dream, Laura realized with dawning horror.

"Me an' my brothers is gonna make you real happy."

Laura began to struggle. He fell on top of her, pressing her down with his superior weight. She flailed at him with her arms, trying to drive him back. But he was strong and agile. After a few seconds of wrestling, he had pinned her arms beneath her.

His breath was foul and hot as he put his lips next to her ear. "Now, I don't want to hurt you. But you fight me, and I'll have to. You hear? I love you, but I know how to handle a woman. I watched my pa beat my ma to make her mind. I'll beat you if I have to."

Laura didn't relax, but she quit fighting him. She had to find some way to wake up her father.

"Now you come with me," the boy said. "You're gonna be real happy at our trailer. It's almost all paid off."

Laura just lay there, wishing she had a weapon.

"Now, I'm gonna let you up. If you make a fuss, you'll be sorry. Okay?"

Laura nodded. She felt his hand relaxing on her mouth. As soon as he had released his grip on her, she bit hard, sinking his teeth into his palm.

The boy gasped but he didn't cry out. Laura started to scream. His other palm came down on her face, slapping her and then blocking off her air.

"I told you not to scream!" he whispered.

Her wide eyes peered into the shadows that covered his face. How had he gotten in? Were his brothers with him?

Don't panic, the little voice told her.

"Are you gonna fight me?"

Laura shook her head.

He drawled, "Good. You're gonna be real happy. Now, come on."

With his hand still on her face, he started to drag her toward the front door.

Laura wanted to knee him in the groin, but the angle was wrong. She had to get her fingernails into his eyes. Anything to hurt him, so he would let her go. She had to fight back.

They were almost to the door when he started whispering to her. "Now, I told you, you're gonna be happy with me and my brothers. We ain't as bad as you think. We . . . uhh—"

Suddenly he let go of her. The boy fell to the floor in a lump. Laura lifted her eyes to see her father standing there with a cast-iron frying pan in his hand. He had brained the mouth-breathing hillbilly, bouncing the heavy object off the intruder's head.

"Thank God!" Laura said.

Mr. Hollister gaped breathlessly at the fallen figure. "What happened? I heard a couple of strange noises . . . I got up and saw him dragging you . . . I grabbed the first thing I could to hit him."

Laura quickly explained what had happened at the Greenville store. Her father listened, growing angrier and angrier as he fixed his gaze on the fallen boy.

"Enough of this," he said. "I'm going to call the police right now. Go wake your mother."

Mr. Hollister reached for the wall phone in the kitchen.

Laura was stepping toward her mother's bedroom when she heard him slam down the phone.

She looked back at her father. "What—"

His face had turned ghostly white. "It's dead."

"Oh no."

"Don't panic," he said. "We're getting out of here."

"But he has brothers—"

Mr. Hollister took a deep breath. "It doesn't matter, Laura. Just wake your mother. And then get Junior and Amy. In the meantime, I'll tie up the boy. We can use him for a hostage. If he—"

Mr. Hollister stopped dead in his tracks.

Laura gaped at the pool of blood where the boy had been. "He's gone!"

The front door swung wildly in the wind. They could see where he had broken the lock to get in. Somehow, even after the blow with the frying pan, he had gotten up and escaped. Either that or his brothers had come after him. What if they were out there, waiting in the pitch-black forest . . . ?

Laura's body shook with fear. "They're going to get us. I just know it."

Her father grabbed her arms. "Listen to me. Nobody is going to get us. Now you find your brother and sister. Hurry."

Laura ran into Amy's room and roused her, getting her younger sister into a down parka and a pair of snow boots. Laura led Amy into

Junior's room where they got him out of bed and put on his coat and shoes.

"Where are we going?" Junior asked, rubbing his eyes.

"Home," Amy said reassuringly.

If we make it home, Laura thought, grimly.

They won't hurt you if you fight them, the little voice assured her.

She took Junior and Amy into the living room where her mother and father were scrambling to get ready to leave. Mrs. Hollister looked terrified. She had thrown her coat over her robe and nightgown.

Mr. Hollister put his arms around his wife and then looked at his kids. "We're going to the wagon and we're getting out of here. Don't stop for anything. Is that clear?"

Laura nodded.

Amy frowned at her father. "I'm afraid."

"Me too," Junior said.

"It's all right," Mr. Hollister replied. "Everything's going to be just fine. Now let's get out of here."

They started for the front door. The cold wind hit their faces, making their eyes tear. Mr. Hollister led the way onto the wooden deck. Laura pushed behind him, wondering if the voices had finally deserted her.

Mr. Hollister had taken two steps on the deck when a cracking sound pierced the dark night. Laura saw the muzzle flash from a small caliber rifle. Her father grabbed his shoulder and slumped to the deck on one knee.

"They're shooting at us!" Junior cried.

"Get inside," Mr. Hollister grunted.

Laura pushed Junior and Amy back into the cabin. Mr. Hollister tried to take a step, but he stumbled, dropping to his knee again.

"Help him!" Mrs. Hollister cried.

Laura reached back to lift her father. With her mother's help, she dragged him back into the cabin, slamming the door. But it wouldn't lock.

Her father gaped at the broken latch. "Barricade. Push something in front of it . . ." He slumped to the floor.

Laura understood immediately. "The refrigerator. Quick. Mom, Amy, Junior. Help me!"

Laura began to push the refrigerator toward the broken door. She heard voices outside as the backwoods family called to each other in the darkness. Her mother moved to help her. Junior and Amy also fell in, pushing the heavy appliance across the floor.

"Shove hard!" Laura said with a grunt.

The refrigerator tipped suddenly, thudding in front of the door.

"More," Laura said. "Get the couch."

The four of them began to work together, piling furniture and anything else they could find to block the entrance to the cabin.

Mrs. Hollister put a hand to her mouth.

"What about the glass doors? They can break through them."

They won't hurt you if you fight them.

Find your weapon.

Laura shook her head, unable to understand what the voices were saying. She had to take care of her father first. His shoulder was gushing blood onto the floor. He had also passed out.

"Mom, we've got to stop the bleeding!"

But Mrs. Hollister had gone catatonic. She just stood there, staring at the glass doors. When Laura tried to touch her, she screeched and backed away. She was losing it completely.

Laura looked at Junior, who was gawking at his father's wound. "Get some towels from the bathroom. Now!"

Junior bolted in the direction of the bathroom.

Amy appeared to be on the verge of tears. "What are we going to do?"

Laura took a deep breath. "I'm working on it, sis."

Junior came back with the towels. Laura made a compress, pushing it against her father's wound to stop the bleeding. She had to get him into one of the bedrooms where he would be safe—or at least a bit more comfortable.

"Amy, take Mom into the back bedroom. Junior, help me with Dad."

Amy led Mrs. Hollister into the bedroom. Laura and Junior began to drag their father away from the door. They pulled him into the bedroom and hoisted him onto the bed with great difficulty and a lot of grunting.

"Is Daddy going to die?" Junior asked tearfully.

Laura gently caressed his forehead. "I don't know."

Find your weapon.

"Where?" Laura asked the voice.

But it was silent again.

She ran back into the living room, wondering what she could use to fight with. There had to be something around. But what?

Her blood froze when a coarse voice echoed outside the cabin. "Give us the girl and we'll let you be."

She started to turn back toward the bedroom, then hesitated when she saw the Ouija board lying on the floor in front of her.

Find your weapon.

She didn't know whether to laugh or cry in frustration as a wave of hysteria threatened to over come her. "All right, great spirits, tell me what to do."

Slowly, deliberately, the triangular piece began to move across the board by itself. Laura's eyes grew wide. She could not believe what she was seeing. The planchette was spelling some message to Laura from the great beyond.

ELEVEN

Laura's dark eyes were riveted to the moving pointer as it jumped under its own power from letter to letter, spelling out its bizarre message. She thought it had to be a trick, maybe the wind or something. Or had she finally snapped under the pressure of knowing that the junk-truck family was outside, stalking her own family? Desperately, she reached for the Ouija board but an electric shock went up her arm, preventing her from touching it. The triangular piece kept moving on the board.

She repeated the letters softly. "F-I-G-H-T."

The pointer stopped on the letter "T."

"Fight?" Laura muttered. "How can I fight them? There's four of them. I'm all by myself."

Something from the other side answered her question, spelling out single word. "F-I-R-E."

"Fire, but I—"

The pointer jumped twice more. "J-R."

"JR? What does that mean? How . . . wait a minute. Junior!"

The pointer remained still.

"Junior? But he—oohh!"

An old memory flashed in her mind. She saw Junior in the backyard two years earlier. He held a can of spray paint in his hand. Laura had seen him spray the stream of paint against a lit match. The result had been a jet of hot flame, leaping out a couple of feet from the nozzle of the spray can. Junior had gotten into a lot of trouble for that.

Laura felt a certain strength in the moment of inspiration. "Of course! That would do it."

She looked at the board. "But where will I find a can of spray paint?"

The indicator didn't move. The spirits of the netherworld had deserted her. She was alone again, left to fight them by herself. With fire.

Outside, in the windswept night, the voices rose again.

"Get her, Paw!"

"They hurt Jacob!"

"Go on, Paw, get her!"

They were drawing closer.

"Jacob's bleedin', Paw."

"She can't do nothin' to us."

"Make her pay, Paw."

"Yeah, we'll take her back to the trailer."

Fire, Laura thought.

She had to trust the spirits and find something to use as a blowtorch. She never consid-

ered questioning the wisdom of the Ouija board.
It was her only chance for survival.

Moving through the house, her head turned
from side to side, looking for a weapon that
would launch a jet of flame. She darted into the
kitchen, throwing open the cabinets. There was
no spray paint in the cabin, nothing to help her.
The broom closet was empty, except for an old
broom and a dustpan. But she wasn't ready to
give up.

Dropping to her knees, Laura started to rum-
mage through the storage space under the
kitchen sink. She couldn't find a thing, at least
until the empty spray bottle fell out onto the
floor. It was the kind of sprayer that could be
used to shoot a long stream or a misty cloud,
the type her mother used to dampen house-
plants.

Close, but not good enough.

As she rose to her feet, she listened again,
trying to detect the voices of her tormentors.
The wind had picked up, roaring through the
forest and rattling the storm shutters. Laura
couldn't hear them anymore. Were they closing
in on the cabin?

Fire!

Now she had to find something to fill it. But
there was nothing under the sink. Laura hurried toward the bathroom. She stepped into the
hallway to see Amy standing there with tears in
her eyes, her face drawn and pale.

"Laura—"

"Amy, go back in there with Mom and Dad."

"Laura, I'm afraid."

Laura touched Amy's shoulder. "So am I, honey. Now, go back in there and keep quiet. Okay?"

"Daddy's going to be okay, isn't he?"

Laura choked back tears. "Yes, he is. Now, you have to stay put. Okay?"

Laura led her little sister back into the bedroom where her family huddled in the darkness. Her father's shallow breathing was barely audible. He lay with his head in her mother's lap. Mrs. Hollister sat on the bed, staring off into space.

"Damn those men," Laura muttered.

She closed the bedroom door and stepped down the hallway to the bathroom.

The medicine cabinet did not offer any promise. Nor did the linen closet. Again, she dropped to her knees, digging into the storage cabinet beneath the bathroom sink. Her hopes plummeted until she reached way back into the shadows, touching something cold and metallic.

Laura drew out the can of room deodorizer, reading the warning label: *EXTREMELY FLAMMABLE. KEEP AWAY FROM FIRE OR FLAME.* She threw down the useless spray bottle and scrambled to her feet.

Now she needed a match or something else to ignite the spray. Hurrying back into the living room, she searched around the fireplace until she found a disposable lighter. Laura struck the lighter, adjusting the flame until it was as high as it would go.

"Fire," she muttered.

Holding the lighter away from her, she lit the lighter and sprayed a stream of alcohol through the flame. The volatile liquid ignited, sending a bolt of fire into the air. She had her weapon now.

Laura turned toward the Ouija board. "All right. I have it now. What do I do?"

The pointer began to move immediately, spelling out one word. "A-T-T-A-C-K."

Laura felt cold all over. "Attack? But I—"

The pointer kept moving. "A-T-T-A-C-K."

Laura shuddered as the pointer stopped on the last letter of the word.

She didn't want to leave the cabin. But the board had told her what she needed to do. She had to obey the spirits of the great beyond.

"Attack," she repeated.

But how was she going to leave the cabin to attack them? The door was still barricaded by the refrigerator and the pile of furniture. Sooner or later, the junk-family would try to break through. Maybe the Ouija board was right—it did make sense to take the fight to them. They wouldn't be expecting that.

Her brown eyes focused on the window at the opposite end of the room. The casement had been shuttered to keep out the inclement weather. Laura had to leave by a window. She tucked the propane lighter into the pocket of her jeans and stepped across the living room.

Lifting the window, Laura unlatched the shutter and pushed it open. The stiff wind caught the shutter and slapped it against the side of the cabin. Laura wondered if the junk-family had heard the noise. It didn't matter. She was launching the attack now.

Holding the spray can in her right hand, Laura struggled to climb through the narrow opening. Her face emerged first into the cold night. She rolled out of the cabin, dropping to the deck with a thud.

Rising slowly, she pressed her back against the wall, pricking her ears to the wind. There didn't seem to be any sign of her assailants. Maybe they had left. Maybe they just wanted to scare her family.

No, they would kill them. They had to now that they were in too deep.

Attack!

The voice had popped back into her head. A sudden energy spread over her body. Were the spirits of the netherworld really watching over her? Or was she slowly losing her mind? Whatever—there was no time to think about it now.

He's coming, the voice told her.

Attack! another voice shouted.

Fire.

Laura crept along the outside wall, shuffling gingerly in the snow. She stopped at the corner of the cabin, frozen with fear. As the wind died for a moment, she heard footsteps crunching in the snow.

He's coming.

Her heart was pounding inside her chest. She could hear it beating in her head. One of the junk-men was walking straight toward her. His footsteps were drawing ever closer. He had probably heard the shutter flapping as it bumped against the house in the wind.

The crunching footsteps halted for a moment. Laura reached into her jeans pocket, taking out the propane lighter. With trembling hands, she lifted the spray can in front of her.

Hard footfalls began to crush the snow again. He was stalking slowly, like a barnyard cat after a field mouse, ready to victimize anything that was weaker.

You're not weaker, the voice assured her.

Laura held her breath as she waited for the predator to show himself. He was only a few feet away, moving in the clearing. He stepped off the dirt, thudding onto the deck. She could hear the rustling of his coat as he started to turn the corner.

Fire.

As soon as Laura caught sight of the dark figure in front of her, she lifted the lighter and pressed the trigger of the spray can. A stream of alcohol-rich spray spewed from the nozzle. She struck the lighter but a sudden gust of wind would not let the flame ignite.

"No!"

The jet of deodorizer spray hit Papa Caleb in the eyes. He cried out, grabbing his face with one hand. Laura turned away, trying to flee back to the open window. But she never made it.

Caleb reached out blindly, grabbing her shoulder. She fought him but he was too strong. He had an ax handle in hand, which he used to restrain her.

Don't give up, the voice urged.

Laura felt the ax handle against her throat, blocking off the air as he pulled her against his filthy body. The spray can and lighter were still in her hands. She listened for the voice, which was right there with her.

Fight him!

Caleb's lips brushed her ear, his breath hot and foul on her neck. "You can't escape, you little tramp."

Use your weapon.

Laura's cold fingers kept squeezing the trigger of the spray can. The flammable liquid ran over her hand, and dripped down the old man's pants leg. He didn't seem to notice.

"I was gonna let you marry my boy," he went on in his hateful voice. "But you hurt my Jacob. Now you gotta pay."

Make him pay.

"You hear me, girl?"

Laura's head had begun to spin. The ax handle was cutting off her air. Her lungs ached

for oxygen. She had almost emptied the bottle.
With numb fingers, she tried to flick the lighter.

"I'm gonna kill your old man," Caleb went
on. "Then we're taking all of you women back to
our trailer. You're gonna keep us fed and
happy. You got that, missy? Now come on with
me. And don't fight or I'll have to beat you."

She felt his grip relaxing. The ax handle
eased on her throat for a moment. Laura
turned, pressing the lighter against his knee.
The flame burst to life, igniting the leg of
Caleb's pants.

He cried out in shock, turning in a circle as
the flames spread up his body. Laura took a
step away from him, lifting the spray can and
spewing the rest of the stuff all over him. The
flames grew brighter as the old man's clothing
began to burn.

Laura watched as the father whirled in a
grotesque dance, turning in circles, trying to
put out the flames. As he fell to the ground,
rolling in the snow, he dropped the ax handle.
Laura reached down, picking up the club.

Finish him!

He would have rolled out the fire if Laura
hadn't hit him. She lifted the ax handle, bringing it down on his head. Some unseen force had
possessed her body. Over and over, she repeated the striking motion, clubbing the father's head as the fire began to grow again.

Laura wasn't really aware of the savagery
she had brought on the man. The strange light

had been glowing behind her eyes while she was beating him. As soon as the light faded, she glanced down to see what she had done. The father's body was engulfed in a pool of blood and fire now.

"No," Laura whispered.

The voice was right there: *He would have done the same to you.*

She heard other voices, real voices, rising from the forest. The sons had seen their father fall. Laura threw the ax handle into the trees and rushed back to the window. She climbed into the cabin, closed the shutter, and locked it behind her.

Footsteps echoed on the deck as the sons rushed to their father. Laura almost felt sorry for them—almost. They yelled threats and curses as they dragged the lifeless body away from the cabin.

"You're gonna pay for this!"

"You can't hurt our paw and get away with it."

"We gonna kill you now, missy!"

A strange gleam had come into Laura's eyes. "Fat chance," she muttered as she eased back into the living room.

The Ouija board was sitting there in front of the fire.

Laura looked down at the triangular pointer. "What next?" she asked solemnly.

Slowly, the spirits from the netherworld began to spell out Laura's next move.

TWELVE

The triangle-shaped pointer moved three times, spelling out a single word: "C-A-R."

Laura stood there, waiting for something more. But it didn't come, at least not right away. The pointer lay motionless on the board. The spirits weren't in the mood to reveal anything else.

"Car?" Laura asked. "Is that all? Just car?"

No reply from the other side.

Laura took a deep breath. "Okay, car! What should I do with the car? Should I take it? Run away? What?"

The pointer did not budge.

Laura was starting to feel desperate again. "You can't leave me hanging like this. Tell me what to do. Do I go to the car?"

The triangle lurched suddenly to one side, indicating, "YES."

Laura nodded, half smiling as her spirits began to lift again. "All right. I'll go to the car."

She started to turn away but the pointer began to move.

It spelled out "C-A-R" again for her.

She felt confused. "Yes, of course, I need the car. I'm going to escape, to take my family with me."

The pointer jumped to "NO."

Laura hesitated, back in the dark again. "Then what?"

"C-A-R."

Her anger grew quickly. "I know, car! But what else? What do I do with the car?"

"C-A-R."

Laura sighed. She wasn't sure what it meant. She had to go to the car, the spirits had told her to do it. But then what?

Trust, the little voice told her.

It was best not to think about it. She just had to act. There was no other way. She had to believe in the spirits that were guiding her.

Her brow wrinkled. "Uh-oh. Where did I leave the keys?"

The last time she had seen the car keys was when she had come back from the bus station after dropping off Kimmy. That meant the keys were probably in her red parka. The parka was in her bedroom.

Laura started back toward the bedroom. A shape appeared suddenly in the hallway. At first, she thought one of the brothers had gotten through the door. But it was only Junior, standing there with tears running down his face.

"Laura, I'm scared."

She knelt to comfort him. "Junior, how's Dad?"

Junior wrapped his chubby arms around Laura's neck. "He's breathing. He woke up once, but he couldn't keep his eyes open."

Laura lifted her own eyes to the ceiling. "Let him live. Let us all live. That's the only thing I'm asking."

Junior gawked at her. "Who are you talking to?"

Laura pushed him gently away from her. "Nobody. Go back to Mom and Dad. Stay with them."

"Are you—"

"Just go," Laura replied, giving him a shove.

Junior disappeared back into the dark bedroom.

Laura hurried toward her own bunk. She found her parka on the floor. She reached into the pocket, grabbing the car keys. A cold feeling spread through her entire body.

Wear the coat.

"I—"

You'll need it.

Laura slipped on the red parka, zipping it tightly over her chest. The warmth came back into her. She was seized by an unearthly power. Was she really going out into the spring snow to face a crazed gang of junk-men? Was she going crazy herself?

They can't hurt you.

She remembered the father, lying on the deck in flames. Had she really done that horrible thing? Or was she in her bed back in Port City, trapped in a nightmare from which she would soon awake? No, this was real. She had experienced enough pain to know that.

Move.

She had to get to the car. She found her way through the shadows of the cabin, hesitating when she saw the barricade in front of the door. There was no way out except for the window. What if they were waiting for her there?

Use the glass door, the voice advised her.

"But if I leave them open, won't they come in?"

The pointer moved, but it didn't answer her question. Instead, it formed a lone, cryptic word: "G-U-N."

A knot twisted Laura's stomach. "Gun? What about a gun?"

No reply from the other side.

"Gun? Tell me what that means?"

The ghostly triangle remained still.

After a deep breath, Laura wheeled toward the glass doors. She had to obey the command. The spirits from beyond had not steered her wrong—not yet anyway.

Creeping to the sliding doors, Laura listened for movement on the deck. What if they were waiting outside for her, right beside the door? After all, they had no reason to fear her, one girl against three men.

Even with their father gone, they still out-numbered her. Maybe they were afraid after what she had done to their patriarch. Even so, they'd want revenge on her, to repay violence with violence. There was no turning back for any of them, not now. They had to play it out.

Car.

"All right!"

She was getting used to the voices, although they could be annoying.

Unlocking the glass door, she slid it open, emerging into the bitterly cold night. The wind raged around her, shaking the empty treetops, slicing into the exposed skin of her cheeks. A cruel trick of spring, she thought.

Laura crept along the wall of the cabin, stopping at the corner. She peeked around the edge at the station wagon. The Hollister family car sat amid the flurries, a dark shape in the distance. She had to reach it before the creepy brothers got to her.

Run.

Laura braced herself for the dash across the deck. She burst around the corner, sprinting as fast as her legs would carry her over the layer of snow. She had to stop at the wooden steps that led to the ground, taking them one at a time with slow precision. At the bottom of the steps, her feet hit a patch of ice. Laura lost her balance, sprawling into the snow.

Crawling off the patch of ice, she regained her balance and started toward the station wagon.

As soon as she got close enough to see the tires, she realized that they had been slashed. All four tires were flat, which would keep her from going anywhere. The spirits had been wrong.

Get in the car.

"No, it won't work!"

Do it.

She wanted to cry, but something impelled her to the other side of the station wagon. Laura hurried around the car and climbed in behind the wheel. She slipped the key into the ignition, then lifted her eyes to the dark heavens.

"What now?

Start it up.

She sighed. "Might as well."

Laura turned the key. The engine groaned, trying to come to life. What difference did it make if she got the car going? She couldn't leave, not on four flat tires.

The engine turned over, sparking as it began to roar. Laura sat there, listening to the mechanical din. What were the spirits doing to her? Or was it simply her own madness?

Danger, the voice said obliquely.

"What?"

Headlights.

Laura's stiff fingers fumbled with the light switch. The headlights popped on to reveal the bare tree trunks in front of her. A surge of adrenaline coursed through her body. Something was going to happen, she could feel it.

Gun.

What gun? Laura wanted to scream. Something moved in the headlights. Laura saw one of the junk-truck brothers as he rose in front of the windshield. He had a rifle in hand. The gun was pointed straight at her.

"No!"

The small caliber rifle cracked once. A bullet careened off the windshield. The junk-man took aim again, firing twice more.

Laura slammed the station wagon into gear. The car lurched forward, picking up momentum even on the flat tires. The junk-brother turned to run away but slipped on a patch of black ice. Laura pressed her advantage—and the gas pedal.

The station wagon smashed into the man, driving him back toward the trees. Laura kept her foot on the accelerator, pressing it to the floor. The station wagon barreled through a snow drift, crashing into the trees, pinning him against a tree.

Laura gaped at the dying man as his eyes bulged from his head. He tried to lift the rifle, but he was too far gone. Blood poured from his mouth, streaming onto his chin and chest. He slumped forward, dropping the rifle onto the hood of the car.

Gun.

But Laura didn't heed the voice right away. She tried to pull the car into reverse, only the engine had died. And when she turned the key again, it wouldn't crank. The car was useless now.

Gun, the voice repeated.

Laura climbed out of the car, sinking into the snow. The headlights of the station wagon were still aglow, casting an eerie beam into the bare woods. She saw the rifle lying across the hood of the car.

Laura reached for the rifle. As her hand closed around the stock, a gurgling noise escaped from the mouth of the dying man. He feebly grabbed the gun, lifting his head for a moment to look at her with desperate eyes. Laura froze, wondering if he was strong enough to shoot her.

"Help me," he groaned. "Helll—"

He pulled one last time at the rifle.

Laura watched him go limp, slumping on the car hood again. She wrested the rifle from his grip. His blood had frozen already on the barrel of the weapon. Laura lifted the rifle, wondering how to use it. Guess I'll just aim and pull the trigger and hope for the best, she thought.

She started back toward the cabin, holding the gun in front of her. Now she had the upper hand. The gun was hers and there were only two of them left, unless the father had survived. No, he was dead. She could feel it. She had killed two of them.

And why not? she thought as she trudged through the snow. "They would have done the same to us," she said aloud.

Cautiously, she approached the patch of ice where she had slipped before. She didn't want to fall and shoot herself. She had to save the rifle, to use it against the two remaining brothers.

Careful, the voice warned her.

"I'm being careful," she replied as she took each step in a deliberate fashion. "Careful."

Her feet clomped on the deck as she made her way back to the glass doors. She would retreat into the warmth of the living room to ask the board what to do next. And it would tell her. It would help her to free her family from the terror inflicted by the junk-truck brood. How could such people exist in a sane world?

As she turned the corner, she saw a shadow looming in front of her. It lunged in Laura's direction, arms raised high. She hadn't been expecting the brother to attack from the glass doors.

"Gonna kill you!"

She lifted the rifle in front of her.

His hands closed around the barrel. They began to spin around as Laura fought him. She felt the cold trigger against her finger.

"Let go! Let go, you little—"

She squeezed the trigger once and then again and again. The cartridges exploded and lodged in his chest.

He let go of the rifle barrel and flew backwards against the railing of the deck. Laura squeezed the trigger again but the rifle clicked harmlessly.

Inside the bedroom, she heard her sister and brother scream in terror at the sound of the gunshots.

"It's okay," Laura cried breathlessly, as an agonized cry came from the mouth of the wounded man. He came off the rail, lurching at her again. Did he have enough strength left to hurt her?

Laura used the rifle like a jousting lance. She gave her own mad cry and charged him, spearing him in the chest with the muzzle of the weapon. Her momentum drove him back to the rail again. His hands closed on the barrel in one last desperate gesture. But he could not stop himself from going over the railing. Laura let go of the rifle as he fell.

She heard him smack against the ice at the edge of the pond. But when she peered over the edge, she could not see his body. The shadows were too thick for her to make out his fallen form.

He's dead, the voice told her.

"My God," Laura muttered. "I've killed three of them."

Get inside.

She hurried back into the cabin, closing the glass door, locking it. Before she consulted with the Ouija board again, she went to the back bedroom, checking on her father. He was still alive, but he seemed to be getting weaker. Her mother was in a catatonic trance.

"What happened?" Junior asked.

Amy looked at her with wide eyes. "What are we going to do, Laura?"

I'm going back to ask the spirits that same question, Laura thought.

"Sit still," she told them, "we're leaving soon."

I hope, she added to herself.

As she moved out of the bedroom, she heard a voice that pierced the night. "You can't get away. You hear me! You can't get away!"

It was Jacob. He was still alive.

Laura ran into the living room, gazing down at the Ouija board. "What do I do now? He's still out there."

The spirits had one word of advice for her: "R-U-N."

THIRTEEN

Laura squinted at the Ouija board. "Run? What does that mean?"

The board was quiet again.

Laura exhaled dejectedly, shaking her head in dismay. "This is getting to be too much. I can't run. Where do I run to?"

Again the triangular piece darted back and forth across the board, spelling out the message. "R-U-N."

Tears welled in Laura's dark eyes as she pleaded with the spirits from the other side. "I can't run, don't you understand? I have to stay here with my family to protect them. That crazy boy is outside. He's going to try to hurt us. Can't you see that?"

"R-U-N."

Hot tears began to flow down her face. "Where do I run? How? Do I take my family with me?"

The pointer moved quickly to indicate NO.

157

Laura wiped her cheeks, trying to regain her composure. "Okay, I get it. I don't take them. Will they be okay if I leave them here?"

No movement on the board. The spirits had deserted her again. Why did they clam up when she needed them the most?

"Please," Laura said in a low voice, "tell me what will happen if I run. Will I survive? Will my family survive? Please, give me a clue."

The planchette slid across the Ouija board again, offering another cryptic, one-word message: "B-E-A-S-T."

Laura grimaced. "Beast? Aw, come on, you can do better than that. Tell me what I—"

The pointer spelled out two words, the same offering again: "R-U-N. B-E-A-S-T." It stopped on the letter "T."

Laura put her hands to her temples. "I don't need this."

Trust, the voice told her.

Outside, the boy's hateful words rose above the wind. "You can't get away from me, girl. You hear me? I'm gonna get you."

"Run," Laura whispered.

That much she understood. But what about the "beast" on the board? What did that mean?

Trust.

She had to trust whatever was sending the messages through the Ouija board. The spirits had steered her well—so far. Laura had to wonder if the residents of the netherworld were capable of mistakes.

Run.

She would obey. But before she left, she would take one final look at her family. It might be the last time that she saw them.

Laura eased down the hallway, opening the bedroom door. She could hear her father snoring, an encouraging sign. Junior and Amy sat shivering in a corner. Her mother just sat there, leaning back against the headboard, her vacant eyes focused on something in the shadows.

"I love you," Laura whispered. "I love you all."

No reply came from her besieged loved ones. She felt guilty for having given them a hard time before. They had always been so good to her. Now she hoped she could save their lives. She closed the bedroom door.

Run, the voice urged.

Laura hurried toward the glass door, sliding it open with one quick motion. As the wind slapped her face, she half expected the crazy boy to jump out at her. But he wasn't there. Laura was greeted only by a crescent moon that had risen above the horizon.

Great, she thought, now he'll be able to see me.

For a moment she trembled, experiencing a weakness in her knees. But she had to obey the spirits. Tiptoeing around the deck, she descended the steps to the ground, moving into the clearing where the car had been parked. She could see the station wagon in the moonlight, the dead man still slumped over the hood.

Run!

She began to sprint on the frozen ground, running up the crest of the rise. She picked up speed when the road sloped down on the other side. Laura thought she might fall, but some unseen force kept her on her feet as she flew forward on the bumpy path.

Bare trees and evergreens lined the dirt road, turning it into a tunnel of shadows in the moonlight. Even with the heavenly glow above, Laura could see only a few yards ahead of her. The wind whistled through the limbs and boughs of the treetops, making ghostly noises all around her, like moaning souls on a march to a graveyard.

She had to make it to the main highway. She could flag down a car. Somebody would help her. It couldn't be much farther.

She had to—

Danger!

Something leapt from the snow-covered brush, landing in front of her on the dirt road, blocking her flight. The ugly face stopped her in her tracks. Laura could see the shape of the boy called Jacob. He stood on the trail, clad only in jeans and a sweatshirt. Blood from the wound on his neck had dried on his face and neck, making him look like something that had crawled out of a coffin.

"Leave me alone," she pleaded.

He shook his head. "You ain't goin' nowhere,

girly. You hurt my paw and my brothers. Now you're comin' with me."

Laura sucked in air so cold that it made her lungs ache. She thought she couldn't take another step. Then the boy moved forward, reaching out toward her.

Laura heard the voices again: *Forest.*

Run!

"I'm takin' you back to—huh!"

Laura lashed out, kicking him hard in the knee. As he fell, Laura darted into the trees. Her feet sank immediately into the cushion of snow. Sharp branches scraped her face and body as she fled. It was hard going as she jumped and hopped between the tree trunks.

One word had begun to repeat in her head, creating an eerie rhythm. *Beast!*

What could it possibly mean?

Her feet kept hitting fallen branches and logs hidden under the snow. She tripped several times, barely able to keep her balance. As she started to rise from one of her falls, a hand grabbed her ankle. Jacob was on her, holding her, trying to pull her toward him.

"You can't escape me, girly."

"No!" Laura cried.

Beast.

Laura kicked out at him. The heel of her foot connected with his nose. The boy tumbled backward, landing on his butt. Laura scrambled to her feet again, trying to make her way through the cold thicket.

Beast.

The word would not leave her brain.

The frigid night air cut through her chest like an ice-honed knife as she took a deep breath. But she could not stop. Her pursuer had risen again himself, crashing after her in his clumsy manner. He seemed to be right behind her, but she would not look back for fear of seeing him.

Laura perceived the moon ahead of her between the tree trunks. It seemed to be hanging over a clearing, suspended in the black sky between the stars. Laura rushed out of the woods expecting to find herself in a snow-covered field. Instead, she ran up an incline, almost falling off a rocky precipice that looked down on Indian Pond. The frozen surface of water lay twenty feet below the isolated crag that she had noticed several times during her vacation.

There was no place for her to go. She had to turn back into the woods. To face her attacker head on.

As soon as she took one step in the opposite direction, the boy was there waiting. He stopped, measured the distance, ready to leap. Panic filled her body. She started to slide into hysteria, trembling and crying, unable to focus on his dark shape.

Beast.

"You're gonna pay, missy. You're dead!"

"No!" Laura screamed. "You can't hurt me. They won't let you."

The boy chortled demonically. "They? Ain't no *they*. Just you and me."

Beast. Beast. Beast.

Laura grabbed her throbbing temples with both hands. "Stop it! Do you hear me! Stop it!"

The boy lurched toward her, reaching out.

But he never grabbed Laura.

Beast.

An unearthly bellowing reverberated in the woods. The boy wheeled suddenly toward the crashing sound that filled the cold night air. A dark, charging shape burst between the trees, smashing headfirst into the boy's chest. He buckled, then flew through the air, sailing past Laura and tumbling over the precipice. He landed with a hard crack on the ice of Indian Pond.

Laura froze, looking at the moose that stood its ground in front of her. The animal's head was low, its eyes burning at Laura, reflecting the spectral glow of the moon. Steam issued from its hot, glaring nostrils. But Laura knew the beast would not hurt her.

The voices were suddenly quiet in her head. Laura felt a warmth spreading over her. Her fears had vanished.

The moose bellowed again.

Laura waved at the animal. "Go away."

It did not move.

"Go on, you beast!"

It would take more than a moose to scare her now.

"Get lost!"

The moose reared its head for a moment, but then turned away, stomping clumsily through the forest, leaving Laura by herself.

Laura did not look back at the boy's fallen body. Instead, she started her trek through the woods, heading for the cabin. She had to check on her family.

She shook her head and exhaled. "Some spring break."

The state police came. Laura's father and mother were taken by ambulance to the nearest hospital, forty miles away. Her father had lost a lot of blood and was in deep shock, but he'd live. Her mother was sedated.

It took the state police a while to sort things out. They finally decided that Laura was telling the truth, although she omitted the part about the Ouija board and the sprits in her head. How could she confess such things?

They found the bodies of the dead father and the two brothers. The investigator could not believe Laura had done this herself. She refused to tell them that help had come from the other side. They would never believe her anyway.

Only one thing bothered Laura—with all their searching, they had not found the body of the boy called Jacob. It was believed that he had fallen through the ice to sink into the depths of Indian Pond. They said they would drag for the body as soon as the ice thawed.

But by then, Laura would be long returned to Port City and the halls of Central Academy.

FOURTEEN

Charlie Sherwood bolted from chemistry class when the final bell rang. He pushed his way into the hall, which was full of junior students eager to get home on a sunny Friday in April. Charlie's head began to turn from side to side, swiveling as he looked for a familiar head of dark hair. He was anxious to see his girlfriend.

Spring break had been over for nearly two weeks, but Charlie still had not seen Laura. Like everyone else at Central, he had heard the rumors. Something bad had happened to the Hollister family up in Maine. Laura's father was recovering from some sort of gunshot wound. Her mother was seeing a psychiatrist, along with the rest of the family. Laura had not come back to school right away, choosing to work with a tutor at home.

Charlie thought he saw Laura's long black hair. He ran to the girl, tapping her on the shoulder. But it wasn't Laura. The girl smiled and flirted, but Charlie just frowned and turned away.

He didn't know what was happening. Nobody knew, not even Kimmy. Charlie had tried to call the Hollister residence, but he always got the answering machine, something they had never used before. Several times he had gone by to knock on the door, but no one ever answered, which was creepy.

Charlie didn't care what happened to Laura in Maine. He just wanted to help. He had to tell her that he loved her. He wanted things to be the way they were before spring break.

His eyes scanned the bustling hallway. A rumor had been floating around that Laura had come back to Central this very day. He had been searching for her since the first tardy bell, but he hadn't been able to find her. Was she avoiding him? Even when he had waited outside several of her classes, he had missed her.

"This bites," he whispered.

Charlie feared the worst—Laura's parents had put an end to their relationship. It was over. He had lost her forever.

His eyes lifted to find the dark-haired girl standing at her locker. "Laura!" He ran to her, grabbing her shoulders, looking happily into her brown eyes. "Laura, it's you, you're really back."

Charlie hugged her, but she did not respond. He pushed her away from him, and gazed into a vacant stare. It was Laura, but a very changed

Laura. This glassy-eyed girl was not the same person he had put in the station wagon a month ago.

He was on the verge of tears. "What happened? What did you—"

"It's all right, Charlie. I'm fine." She said in a flat, emotionless voice.

He started to kiss her. Laura turned her cheek. She was limp, lifeless. Something had turned her against him.

"Laura, please, tell me what's wrong?"

She took a deep breath, closed her locker door, and gazed off into the distance. "I—I can't tell you, Charlie. I have to go." Laura started to walk away from him.

"What about the ring?" Charlie challenged.

Laura stopped with her back to him. For a moment, Charlie thought he had a chance to rekindle what they had shared before spring break. But when she turned around to look at him with that blank expression, his spirits sank.

Laura reached into the book bag her mother had given her as a present for her seventeenth birthday. "Here." She thrust a small box at Charlie.

He knew what was in the box. "Why? Is it me? Is it something I did?"

She shook her head. "No, Charlie. It's not you. It's me." She tossed the box at him and started off down the hall.

Charlie caught the ring box in his right hand.

He watched her walk away. A lone tear began to roll down his face. He had lost Laura. And he had no idea why she was breaking up with him.

After her first day back at Central, Laura walked home by herself, avoiding everyone, including Kimmy. The psychiatrist thought that going back to school on a Friday would be good for Laura. She could have one day of classes and then come home to rest on the weekend. After the trauma their family had suffered, all of the Hollisters would need some time to recover. The doctor said it might be a few years before they approached a normal family life again.

When Laura returned to the house on River Run Lane, she entered slowly, listening for sounds of life. Her mother had taken to staying in the kitchen most of the time. She cooked and cleaned compulsively, saying very little to anyone. She felt guilty that she hadn't helped more at the cabin, when the horrible men attacked them from the darkness.

Laura tiptoed past the kitchen, heading for her father's room. He was lying on the bed, reading the newspaper. Jim Hollister had taken sick leave from the shipyard to recuperate. He was the only one in the family who seemed to be getting better.

"Hi, Dad," Laura said timidly.

He nodded and smiled. "How was school?"

She shrugged. "Okay. Are Junior and Amy home?"

"In their rooms. Dinner's in a couple of hours. I bet you have a lot of homework. Don't you?"

"Yes. I'm going upstairs."

It was only when she closed the door to her bedroom that Laura felt truly safe from the horrors of the world. After defeating the men at the lake, she had experienced a short period of elation, of triumph. But then the feelings of shame and disgust came over her, the wicked realization of what she had done. She had not been prepared for the depression and the nightmares, seeing their ugly faces in her dreams.

She tossed her book bag on the bed and turned toward her vanity table, where the Ouija board sat in front of the mirror. The board had not moved since its last message about the beast. Nor had she heard the voices in her head. It was all so disappointing. Laura *wanted* the voices to speak to her, to have the board tell her that everything would be all right. She had come to rely on those spirits who had guided her so well.

But it just sat there, motionless. No matter how obsessively she stared at the board and the triangular pointer, it would not respond. The spirits had helped her through the worst, but they were gone now. And nothing could change the way Laura felt. Would she ever recover?

She sat on the edge of the bed, gazing at the

board with her dark irises. "Just one letter," she said. "Just a yes or a no. Anything."

But the spirits apparently weren't home.

Laura lay back on her bed, gazing up at the white ceiling of her bedroom. What was going to happen to her? When would the horrible feeling go away? Would she be lost in this melancholy mood forever? How could she get out of it?

For the rest of the afternoon, she stayed in bed, watching as the shadows lengthened over her room. Night was overtaking Port City this Friday night, when all of her friends would be going out to have a good time. But not Laura.

She had to find her concentration. She had to recover some semblance of normalcy in order to feel human again. She hated what she had done to Charlie. But what choice did she have? Her heart was empty. She had *killed* three people.

She sat up on her bed. She had to do something. Her father had been right about one thing—she had plenty of homework. She was at least a week behind, even after the sessions with a tutor.

Laura switched on the light next to her bed. Opening the book bag, she began to sift through the texts and papers. She grimaced and shook her head. She had forgotten her algebra book, leaving it behind in her locker. It was the subject that needed the most attention. She had planned to work all weekend to catch up, but Charlie's appearance at her locker had thrown her.

What was she going to do?

She sighed. "Back to school," she said to herself. "I hope I can still get in." She'd have to walk there and back before dinner.

Laura started for the front door. She didn't notice that the pointer on the Ouija board had begun to move. The triangular piece jumped suddenly, sliding to the word NO.

FIFTEEN

Central Academy sat at the end of Rockbury Lane, dark and silent with only a few security lights to illuminate the outer campus. A cool wind blew over Port City, bringing an eerie mist from the Tide Gate River. Laura walked briskly down Rockbury, pushing through the mist that formed halos around the street lamps that glowed overhead. The river mist, which Laura had known all her life, left an unpleasant dampness on her smooth face.

When she reached the edge of the Central campus, Laura stopped for a moment, gazing toward the junior classroom building. A weird sensation filled her, a feeling similar to the sense of anticipation she had experienced in the Maine woods. The school was suddenly forbidding, threatening, foreign.

Laura shook her head and breathed in the moist night air. This had to stop. She couldn't be afraid forever. She had come to Central to get her algebra book. It didn't matter that the eerie fog was growing thicker or that she could hear every sound the night had to offer. She had to take control of her own life again. Laura was a student and students had to do homework.

Laura moved through the fog as it swirled around her, heading for the junior wing of Central Academy. As she walked forward, her footsteps echoed in the mist. Then, for a moment, she thought she heard a second set of footsteps matching her own. She stopped abruptly, listening in the fog. But there were no sounds in the night, save her own breathing. She pushed on again.

"*Laura. . . .*"

Her body stiffened to a halt. She had heard someone call her name. It had rung clearly in her ears.

Had the voices come back in her head?

The mist washed over her as the foghorn from a tug on the river reverberated from the east. It only sounded like her name. There was nothing to fear.

"Just get the book and go home," she told herself.

She worried momentarily that she wouldn't be able to get into the junior wing of the school. But as she drew closer to the building, she saw that a side door had been propped open with a broom. The janitor had been mopping the hallway. Laura stood at the door, gazing down the line of lockers on the wall. The dim security lights rendered a purplish haze on the interior of the building.

"*Laura. . . .*"

She glanced back over her shoulder for a moment. Had that been the foghorn? Something seemed to be moving in the mist behind her. No, it was only the rolling cloud of fog.

Get the book and go home!

Laura started into the hall, stepping gingerly on the damp floor. Her locker was in the middle of the corridor. She opened it and retrieved the algebra textbook, then locked it quickly so she could leave in a hurry.

As she turned away from the locker, she heard her name again. "*Laura. . . .*"

She peered toward the opening at the end of the corridor. A dark figure appeared in the doorway, framed by the mist and the aura of the security lights. Laura took a step backward. A heavy hand fell on her shoulder.

"No!" she cried.

"Hey, it's all right, little lady. Calm down."

Laura was face to face with a man in a khaki uniform. The janitor held a mop in his other hand. Laura drew away from him, trembling.

The kindly, gray-haired man smiled at her. "Sorry. Didn't mean to scare you. Are you all right?"

Laura nodded and then glanced back at the open doorway. The dark shape had disappeared—if it had ever been there in the first place. Was her imagination running wild?

"You know you shouldn't be in here after four o'clock," the janitor went on. "Not without special permission. I'm supposed to call the police when I catch a trespasser."

"Call them," Laura replied. She would have welcomed a policeman just now.

The janitor chortled. "No, you look harmless. After a book, were you?"

"Yes, but you can—"

"No, I won't call them. You seem like a good kid. Take your book and go on home."

Laura shuddered. "Would you—I mean, could you walk me to the end of the hall?"

He nodded. "Okay. Sorry I scared you."

As the janitor strode beside her, he babbled on about nothing. Laura's eyes were darting back and forth, anticipating dark shapes. One thought kept running through her mind: They never found the body. Could Jacob still be alive? What if he had come back from the dead? After all the bizarre things she had endured over spring break, it wasn't out of the realm of possibility.

The janitor sent her out into the misty night with a warning. "You go straight home, young lady. This isn't a fit night for anyone to be out."

She started to say something but he closed the door in her face.

"Laura. . . ."

Her heart leapt into her throat. Turning to

her left, she gazed into the mist. Were those footsteps rising on the night air? Something seemed to be moving in the fog, coming straight at her.

"*Laura. . . .*"

The foghorn sounded. Laura ran across the campus as fast as her feet would carry her. She made it to Rockbury Lane without stumbling. She hurried under the streetlights, certain that she was being followed.

On the way home, she avoided Fair Common Park, sticking to the busy streets that were well lit. As she approached the entrance to Prescott Estates, she heard the rumbling of a large vehicle. A truck passed in front of her. For a moment, she thought she saw the flash of an orange hunting cap.

"No!"

But it was only a street sweeper for the city, guiding his truck along the curb. All city employees wore bright orange hats and vests. It was part of their uniform.

Laura rushed home to River Run Lane. Her family was sitting around the dinner table when she walked it. Laura's face was ashen. Her father asked if she was all right. Laura just nodded. What could she tell them? That she was seeing things again? That the boy in the orange cap had come back from the grave to haunt her? She sat at the table and tried to eat, but had no appetite.

When dinner was over, Laura went upstairs

with her algebra book. She didn't notice the shift in the Ouija board planchette. For the rest of the night, she tried to get a grip, to study. She was actually starting to make progress when she began to feel sleepy. Lying back on the pillow, she closed her eyes, praying that she could get a full night's sleep without the nightmares bothering her.

But the dreams came anyway. The boy was there, holding his hand over her mouth, saying hateful things to her. Laura opened her eyes, escaping one nightmare to find another.

"Hello, Laura."

The boy called Jacob was there, hovering over her. She tried to scream but his hand was covering her mouth. He had come in through the bedroom window. Mist poured into her room from the opening.

"You killed my paw and my brothers," he said in a hoarse whisper. "You tried to kill me, but I was too strong. You know how long it took me to find you? I had to go back to the cabin after everyone was gone. I went through the trash until I found your address. I came to Port City to find you, Laura. Now you're going back with me. Me and you is gonna get married, just like I said before."

Laura felt paralyzed. It had to be a dream. No, she felt the cold air on her skin. She smelled the horrible stench of this monster.

His other hand tightened around her throat.

"You make one sound and I'll snap your neck like a twig. You hear me?"

But Laura felt everything fade away all of a sudden. The light had begun to glow behind her eyes. She could hear the scraping of the Ouija board planchette on the other side of her bedroom.

The voice rushed back into her head: *Finish him*. Relief threatened to overwhelm her; the voices hadn't deserted her.

"Let's go," Jacob told her, lifting her from the bed.

Laura felt a new strength surging through her body. As his grip relaxed a little, she lashed out with her arms, pushing him off her.

A maniacal screech erupted from the boy's mouth. "I'm gonna kill you!"

He charged, but Laura managed to avoid him. She started for the door but he was too quick. His hands fell on her shoulders, pulling her back toward the vanity table. Laura felt his fingers on her throat.

"Kill you!"

She bumped against the vanity as he began to choke her. The Ouija board pointer was directly behind her. Laura reached back, grabbing it in her right hand.

"Killed my paw. Killed my brothers. Kill you!"

Laura's head grew lighter as he choked her. *Finish him*!

With the last of her strength, Laura swung

the pointer from behind her back. She stabbed him in the neck, hitting his jugular vein. Jacob cried out, letting go of her. He struggled to pull the pointer from his body, but it wouldn't dislodge.

His face contorted into a look of rage and disbelief. Blood spurted around the triangular shape. His hands could not pull it away.

Laura's eyes grew wide as she watched Jacob die. Suddenly, the pointer burst into flames and fire rose all around the boy's head. He slumped to the floor, twitching.

The door to Laura's bedroom burst open. Her father rushed in to witness the ghostly spectacle. The flames around the boy's head subsided. Jacob twitched a few more times, then lay still.

Laura smiled strangely at her father. "It's over," she said softly.

Mr. Hollister reached out to his daughter.

But Laura's eyes rolled back in her head. She slumped to the floor next to the body of the dead boy.

She was free now.

EPILOGUE

Laura opened her eyes to the bright glow of fluorescent lights. She had been at Port City Community Hospital for two days, recovering from the events of the past month. Some doctor, a psychiatrist from Rochester, had suggested that Laura should be observed for a couple of days in her present condition.

The only problem was that Laura did not know what her condition was. She had awakened in a private room, feeling, for all intents and purposes, normal again. She had no recollection of the spring break or what had happened thereafter. It was all a mystery to her. Why was everyone making such a fuss? There was nothing wrong with her.

Her father came into focus. He smiled at her. Why was his arm in a sling? Why did he seem so worried about her? And why wasn't her mother here with him?

"Hi, Princess," he said in a kind voice. "You've been resting well, they tell me."

Laura sighed, scratching her upturned nose. "I guess. When are they going to let me go home, Dad? I hate it here. They keep gawking at me like I'm crazy."

His brow wrinkled with a look of concern. "Laura, don't you remember anything?"

She took a deep breath, sitting up in the adjustable bed. "We were getting ready to go to Maine. That's the last thing I remember. You and Mom were mad at me. Hey, where's Mom?"

Jim Hollister's expression grew more dire. "Uh, she's at home. We've all been through a lot, honey."

Laura's eyes narrowed. "We have? What happened? I just don't have a clue, Dad."

He patted her hand. "Get some rest."

"I don't need any rest! I want to see my friends. I want to go back to school. Where's Kimmy? And Charlie?"

"They thought you shouldn't have any visitors for a couple of days," her father replied. "But . . . wait a minute. I'll see what I can do."

He left the private room. A duty nurse came in and tried to give Laura a pill. She refused to take it. The nurse left in a huff. Laura leaned back and sighed.

"What the heck is going on?" she wondered aloud.

An unbearable hour later, her father returned with a smile on his face. "There's somebody here who wants to see you."

The sandy-haired boy appeared with his sparkling green eyes and a sheepish grin. "Hi, there," he said tentatively.

Laura held out her arms. "Charlie—come here!"

He ran to her and embraced her, pressing his lips to hers.

Mr. Hollister blushed. "I'll leave you two alone."

Laura gazed into his eyes. "I love you."

Charlie could not believe his good fortune. "I love you, too. When you gave me that ring back I—"

A horrified expression stretched over Laura's face. "I gave you back the ring? No wonder they locked me away. Where is it?"

Charlie pulled the box from his pocket. "Are we going steady again? I mean—"

Laura ripped the box from his hand and took out the ring, slipping it on her finger. "It's so beautiful. Kiss me again."

After their lips met, Charlie gaped at her. "What happened? You were a different person when you came back from spring break."

Laura shook her head. "I have no idea. One minute I was saying good-bye to you, the next second, I'm here in this bed. Everything in between is a blank."

There was a knock at the door.

"Anybody home?"

Kimmy stuck her head into the room.

Laura waved at her. "Get over here!"

They were together again, laughing, talking, just like old times. It was great to see them. Laura couldn't wait to get back to classes at Central Academy.

"So," Kimmy said finally, "have you enjoyed your birthday present from me?"

Laura frowned. "Birthday present?"

"The Ouija board?" Kimmy replied. "Don't tell me you've forgotten already!"

Laura stiffened. "What Ouija board?" Then, for a moment, a dull light appeared behind her eyes and she heard a tiny voice in her head.

Good-bye, Laura.

But everything faded quickly. She was back for good. She asked Charlie to kiss her again. Then she grinned at Kimmy and asked for all the latest gossip from the halls of Central Academy.

WELCOME TO CENTRAL ACADEMY . . .

It's like any other high school on the outside. But inside, fear stalks the halls—and terror is in a class by itself.

———————

Please turn the page for a sneak preview of the next TERROR ACADEMY BOOK—don't miss THE NEW KID!

Nan Easterly's hazel eyes scanned the Central Academy gymnasium, searching for an empty seat on the hard, wooden bleachers. Most of the lower seats were taken already, mainly because a single section of the bleachers had been pulled out for the assembly. Nan gazed upward to the higher rows, searching for Debbie, her best friend. It was the first day of school at Central and all the sophomores had to attend a special orientation before they started classes.

"Where are you, Debs?" Nan said to herself.

Debbie had promised to meet Nan at the corner of Taylor and Washington Streets before school, but she hadn't arrived in time to walk to Central with Nan, so Nan had left without her. Nan had walked all the way from Pitney Docks by herself. Debbie didn't live in Pitney Docks. Her father was a doctor so her family lived in Prescott Estates, the best neighborhood in Port City.

Nan sighed and shook her head. She had only known Debbie since the summer but they were fairly close. Still, Debbie was often late whenever they got together. Nan hadn't really expected Debbie to come all the way over to Taylor Street to meet her, even after Debbie had promised. It would have been nice, though, to have a friend next to her. Nan needed a friend on her first day at Central Academy. She had attended Rochester High as a freshman, so Central was new to her.

Being a new kid stunk, Nan thought to herself. Why had her parents moved into Port City? Her father had said something about buying a house in a poor neighborhood that was on the upswing. But Nan only knew that she had left her few friends behind to come to a school where nobody knew her—except Debbie, and she was nowhere to be seen.

Someone bumped into Nan, almost knocking her to the parquet floor of the gym. She managed to keep her balance long enough for a pair of strong hands to steady her. When she turned toward a sandy-haired boy, he smiled warmly at her.

His tone was friendly, too. "Hi there."

Nan blushed and tried to smile back. "Hi," she said in a timid voice.

The boy gave her an up-and-down glance. Nan was dressed in jeans, running shoes, a white blouse and a brown corduroy vest. She had never considered herself particularly attractive, but the boy had quickly noticed her wholesome looks. Her short brown hair had a natural wave and streaks of auburn. She was tall and slender, and her figure was graceful, like a dancer. Her smooth face was unblemished and she had high cheekbones and a thin nose. At fifteen, soon to be sixteen, she was beginning to blossom, though she had hardly noticed.

The boy kept grinning at her. "I'm Jimmy. Jimmy Chambers."

Nan gave a nod and looked away. "Uh-huh."

"I'm going out for football," he went on. "You know, you could try out for cheerleader."

Nan offered an indifferent sigh, all the while noticing that he was really cute. Soft brown eyes, a pearly smile, sandy bangs hanging over his tanned forehead. He was clad in a pink, button-down shirt, brown chinos, and a pair of penny loafers—a preppy type, not at all what she had gotten used to at Rochester High. Why had her parents moved into Port City?

Jimmy Chambers would not go away, but stood there gawking and smiling. "Orientation's a drag, huh?"

Nan didn't want to be impolite, but she wasn't in the mood for a conversation. All around them, the throng of sophomore students buzzed with anticipation of the school year, trying to get settled before the eight o'clock bell. It wasn't the time or place to start an intimate exchange, even with someone as hunky as Jimmy Chambers.

He had no intention of letting her escape.

"Are you new at Central? I haven't seen you before."

Nan shrugged. "Uh-huh." She continued to search for Debbie who was nowhere in sight.

"Where'd you go last year?" he asked, determined to make the connection.

Nan couldn't find the words, so she tried to ignore him. She wanted to talk, but it was all wrong. Why had he come along just now with his boyish enthusiasm?

"Rochester?" he asked. "Did you go there?"

"Uh, yes, Rochester."

When she looked away, he maneuvered around, trying to make eye contact. Nan found herself gazing into his brown, sparkly irises. She was about to say something more encouraging when a set of red fingernails appeared on Jimmy's shoulder.

"Sorry little girl," a female voice said, "he's taken."

Nan saw a flash of golden hair and a pair of blue eyes staring back at her. A pretty blonde girl had come out of the crowd to claim Jimmy as her prize. She was dressed in a tight-fitting red sweater and a white skirt. Nan disliked her immediately and would have probably disliked her even if they hadn't been competing for Jimmy's attention.

Jimmy rolled his eyes. "This is Ginger."

Ginger brandished a catty smile. "Hello."

Nan wanted to crawl under a rock. She was embarrassed at Ginger's obvious attempt to stake out her territory. Nan had never had a boyfriend before, but she figured she wouldn't be so possessive if she was lucky enough to hook up with someone.

Jimmy kept smiling. "Uh, Ginger, this is—hey, you haven't told me your name."

"And she isn't going to," Ginger replied, grabbing Jimmy's arm. "Good-bye."

Nan watched as Ginger dragged Jimmy away from her. Some nerve, Nan thought. She was tingling all over from the weird encounter. It was a strange sensation that had come over her a lot lately, a feeling of anticipation and dread, a counterpoint of happiness and sadness with a multitude of other emotions welling through her at the same time.

"Hey, Easterly, there you are!"

She looked up to see Debbie coming straight toward her. Debbie's jet black hair bounced on her shoulders. She was dressed all in black—jeans, leotard top, shoes and sunglasses. Like Nan, Debbie was a new kid in Port City, having moved to the quaint, seaside New England town from Pennsylvania. They had met at Hampton Way Beach in July.

Nan's pretty face wrinkled into a look of disbelief. "What happened to you? Are you going to a funeral?"

Debbie smiled, taking off the sunglasses to reveal her bright blue eyes. "Great, isn't it. I thought I'd give these geeks something to look at."

Nan felt a little awkward because everyone in the first two rows in front of them had begun to stare at Debbie.

Debbie, who was shorter and heavier than Nan, scowled at them. "Take a picture for the yearbook," she quipped. "It'll last a lot longer."

Nan blushed again. "Debbie!"

Debbie grinned. "Off to a great start."

Nan grabbed her arm. "Come on, let's find a seat."

At that moment, the loudspeaker crackled to life and the public address system blared feedback into the gym. "Please take your seats, students." Harlan Kinsley, the assistant principal of Central Academy, stood on the stage at the other end of the basketball court.

"We'd better sit down," Nan said.

Debbie sighed. "I hate school. I hated school back in Pittsburgh and this doesn't look any better."

"Come on, I don't want to get in trouble on our first day," Nan replied. "Let's go up there where the empty seats are."

They found an aisle that led to the higher tiers. Nan let Debbie go first. Everyone looked at them as they passed. They were certainly a strange pair with Nan in her white blouse, a towering, slender figure over Debbie's chubby, black-clad frame.

As they climbed to the top, Nan caught the face of Jimmy Chambers, gawking expectantly at her from the seats. She blushed when he winked at her. It was clear that he liked Nan, a certainty that boosted her ego tremendously. But then she saw Ginger glaring daggers and the rapturous feeling faded a little.

She wondered if Debbie had noticed that Jimmy was looking in their direction. Why couldn't she take Jimmy away from the brassy blonde type? Maybe he wanted a girl who was less flashy.

"There," Debbie said. "Let's park it before the vice-principal has a cow."

As soon as they were sitting on the bleacher tier, Nan cast a cautious look downward, searching again for Jimmy. Sure enough, he was gazing up at her over his shoulder. Nan found herself smiling to encourage him.

Debbie had noticed all right. "Not bad, Nan. Who is he? And who's that model-girl with him?"

"His name is Jimmy Chambers," Nan replied.

Debbie chortled. "Wow, you work fast. What about the babe? Is that his girlfriend?"

"She seems to think so," Nan replied.

"Oohh, major hunkage," Debbie went on. "Maybe this place isn't so bad after all."

"I guess not," Nan said dreamily.

But then the face of the blonde girl turned up to glare at her again. Ginger made Jimmy look back at the stage, where the assistant principal was getting ready to give his speech. After one last hateful look, Ginger showed Nan the back of her blonde head.

Nan experienced a sudden urge to retaliate. But what could she do? Judging by the crowd around Jimmy and Ginger, they were obviously two of the most popular students in the sophomore class. And what was Nan? A new kid!

"Welcome to Central Academy," the assistant principal began. "My name is Harlan Kinsley—"

Nan slumped on the seat next to Debbie. She felt horrible all of a sudden. Her orientation at Central had finally begun.

The tall boy in the leather jacket had been wandering south for nearly two days. In the morning light, he ambled along the side of the road, never thinking once about sticking out his thumb to hitch a ride. His head was muddled, foggy, incapable of any recollection beyond the days of walking. A dull gleam in his light brown eyes gave him a stunned expression that had worried the man at the convenience store in Lewiston, where the boy had purchased a couple of hot dogs and a carton of orange juice. Everyone seemed to fear an aimless drifter with no apparent purpose to his journey.

Stopping on the side of the highway, the boy slumped to the ground, sitting on the cushion of wildflowers. September still bathed the New England countryside in warm, bright sunlight. His lusterless eyes lifted to the blue sky, as if he were searching for an answer to the many

questions that swirled in his head. He ran a
hand over the unruly cap of brown hair, asking
himself the same questions over and over.

Who am I?

Where did I come from?

*Where did I get the wad of money in my coat
pocket?*

Reflexively, he touched the tender spot on his
forehead. The bruise was small with a slight
abrasion on the skin. There had been a little
blood on the wound, but he had washed it off in
the rest room of a gas station. The attendant at
the station had given him a cautious glance
when he handed him the key to the rest room.

Where am I going?

How did I get here?

Did I do something wrong?

Who hit me on the head?

So far, the tall boy hadn't spoken a word to
anyone during the journey. He wondered if he
even had a voice. Yet, there had been no need to
speak. Just a need to walk south.

Why south?

He had stared at his reflection in the window
of a restaurant along the way. He wore a long,
leather jacket, dirty jeans and a gray T-shirt
with holes in the fabric. The boots on his feet
appeared to be fairly new and evenly polished.

Where had the boots come from?

Am I running from something?

Or running to something?

Maybe both.

Why am I walking south?

What happened to put me here?

He felt the cool breeze on his handsome face. A couple of times during his journey, he had received encouraging glances from pretty girls. But he had ignored their batting eyes. He surrendered to the urge to keep moving, to walk south toward—what?

Did I hurt someone?

Did someone hurt me?

Why do I feel like someone or something is after me?

Reclining on the bed of wildflowers, he let his eyes stray to the sky again. His only emotion was an intense sense of urgency that overwhelmed everything in his head. He couldn't shake it. Yet, he had no memory of anything to dread or fear.

Maybe if I sleep, I'll remember.

He closed his brown eyes. A dark wave swept over him, blocking the light. His slumber was dreamless, like a coma. But when he awoke, he opened his eyes to the threat of trouble.

Black silhouetted shapes had come between his eyes and the sky. Two uniformed figures stood over him. He tried to sit up but the sole of a boot pressed against his chest, pushing him back to the ground. The highway patrol officers kept him from rising.

"Stay put," a deep voice warned.

The other officer began to pat the boy's pockets. "He's clean. No weapons." His voice was higher.

The boy tried to focus on their faces but his eyes refused to cooperate.

The boot left his chest. "Okay," said the deep voice, "I'm going to let you up. But you're going to move slowly. Do you understand me?"

The boy nodded absently. He didn't care what they did to him. Maybe they could solve the mystery inside his brain.

The higher voice accused him. "He could be the one who escaped from the correctional institute over in Lewiston."

The deep voice disagreed. "Nah, that guy was a lot older. This kid can't be much more than eighteen or nineteen. How old are you, son?"

He wondered if he could speak. "I—I don't know." He heard the tenor pitch of his own voice.

"Geez," said the high voice, "he's a nutcase."

"Maybe. Where are you going, kid?"

"I—I don't know."

The tall boy wondered if those were the only words in his head. He hadn't been required to speak until now, had no memory of ever speaking. He didn't want to do anything except keep moving south.

A hand was extended to him. "Get up," said the high voice.

Both officers helped him to his feet.

Deep voice: "He's hurt, look at that strawberry on his forehead. It's a beaut."

"You in pain, boy?"

He shook his head.

"Any I.D.?" the high one asked.

He sighed. "I don't know."

"Guess we better take him in," said the deep voice. "Come on."

They put him in the back of the patrol car, driving him to the state police substation off the interstate. The tall boy wasn't scared. He sat under the fluorescent lights, sipping soda and nibbling on a doughnut, staring blankly at the walls. Then they took his fingerprints and waited a long time before they called him into another room.

"You're clean, kid," a captain told him. "I can't hold you here. I could take you over to the juvenile detention center if you're under eighteen. Are you under eighteen?"

"No," the tall boy replied, not sure if he was telling the truth about his age.

He just wanted to get south.

"You got any money?" the captain asked.

The boy nodded.

"Let me see."

Reaching into the pocket of his leather jacket, the boy pulled out a wad of crumpled bills.

The captain's eyes grew wider. "Good Lord, you must have a couple of hundred bucks there. Where'd you get it?"

The boy shrugged. "I don't know."

The captain pointed a finger at him. "You know, I could hold you, put you in the hospital for observation."

"I—I don't care," the boy replied.

Something began to gnaw a hole in the boy's gut. He really didn't want them to hold him now, but he had to bluff. If the bluff worked, he could head south. He had to get south.

Why south?

He couldn't show fear or they wouldn't let him go.

The captain sighed. "Boy, you're a real piece of work. Are you sure you haven't done something wrong somewhere?"

The tall boy in the leather jacket remained silent.

"How'd you get that lump on your forehead?"

No reply, just a glance into space with the glassy brown eyes.

The captain shook his head. "Okay, I'm gonna have them take you to the bus. With that kind of money, you should be able to get out of town. I don't want to see you around here again."

The boy nodded.

Two different officers took him to the bus station, dropping him at the entrance. He entered the terminal, gazing up at the schedule on the wall. One name jumped out at him from the southbound column—Port City.

That sounded right.

But why?

He didn't care.

He bought a one-way ticket and sat down to wait for the bus.